GREEK TRAGEDY: AN INTRODUCTION

Current and forthcoming titles in the Classical World Series

Classical World Series

GREEK TRAGEDY: AN INTRODUCTION

Marion Baldock

Bristol Classical Press

General Editor: John H. Betts
Series Editor: Michael Gunningham

This impression 2006
First published in 1989 by
Bristol Classical Press
an imprint of
Gerald Duckworth & Co. Ltd.
90-93 Cowcross Street, London EC1M 6BF
Tel: 020 7490 7300
Fax: 020 7490 0080
inquiries@duckworth-publishers.co.uk
www.ducknet.co.uk

A catalogue record for this book is available
from the British Library

ISBN 1 85399 119 8
EAN 9781853991196

Printed and bound in Great Britain by
CPI Antony Rowe Ltd, Chippenham

Cover illustration shows the death of Aegisthus,
from a calyx-krater by the Dokimasia Painter
[drawing by Christine Hall]

Contents

List of Illustrations

Introduction

What is the essence of Greek tragedy – spectacle, poetry, emotion or a combination of all three? The plays were usually based upon myths, powerful and familiar representations of human dilemmas – conflicts between men and gods, between members of a family or between citizen and state. Although performances were highly stylised and dominated by conventions the audience was drawn into the sufferings of the characters, their hopes, fears, lives and sometimes deaths. The playwrights' poetic and dramatic skill determined the intensity of the audience's involvement. Some critics have spoken of the audience undergoing a *katharsis* – a sort of ritual purging – and Aristotle in the *Poetics* suggested that the arousing of emotions of fear and pity was essential for tragedy. Certainly no one could have been unmoved by the sight of Oedipus who had blinded himself after realising that he had unwittingly committed incest, or by the scene at the end of the Euripides' *Bacchae* when Agave discovers that it is not a lion's head but her son's head which she is holding as a trophy.

What would the audience actually have seen? On certain days in March three tragedies were performed one after another in a huge open air theatre. A chorus, twelve or fifteen in number, was present throughout each performance, weaving intricate patterns on the circular dance floor as they sang and danced the choral odes. The chorus and the actors wore masks complete with a head of false hair and flowing robes. Action was rarely shown on stage – death and disaster were instead described in elaborate messenger speeches, themselves a *tour de force*. Much depended on suspension of belief; there were few props or special effects. No women acted and the number of actors was limited to three per play. The same actor might play several different roles, both male and female, within one play. As there were no programmes everything had to be made clear by the dialogue. The plays were written entirely in verse with complicated metrical patterns and were accompanied by musical instruments.

Does all this seem rather strange and highbrow? It has been compared to a cross between Japanese Kabuki theatre and grand opera.

1

Yet these plays were attended and appreciated by citizens of every social class and were as popular as television 'soap opera' is today! The plays were also part of a religious festival and a competition. There was much rivalry between the playwrights. The impact of the tragedies upon their audiences can be seen from Aristophanes' comedies. He parodied the tragic playwright Euripides in several of them (notably the *Acharnians* and *The Poet and the Women*) and the audience would not have found this amusing unless they remembered well the works of Euripides which were being imitated. Most revealing of all is the *Frogs*, produced by Aristophanes in 405 BC, in which not only is the theme of the play the need for a good tragic poet to save the city from ruin and defeat, but the whole second half of the play is devoted to a mock contest between the two great tragic poets Aeschylus and Euripides. No comic playwright would have produced such a play unless he could rely on his audience being extremely interested in and familiar with the works of Aeschylus and Euripides.

Greek tragedies can be examined and appreciated at many levels, as 'drama' in the Greek sense of the word, a doing or an action, as spectacle, as poetry and as plays with a message. In this book I intend to explain the theatrical conventions of the performances and then to consider how the playwrights exploited these conventions by detailed examination of some of their plays.

Chapter 1
The Performance of Greek Tragedy

The theatre

The tragedies were always performed in the open air and in daylight. The Theatre of Dionysus at Athens, where all of the tragedies which have survived were first staged, was situated on the south-east slopes of the Acropolis, the sacred hill in the centre of Athens. Originally the spectators would have sat on the ground or on banks of wooden seats which were temporarily erected for the performances. Probably the only part of this theatre which was built of stone before the fourth

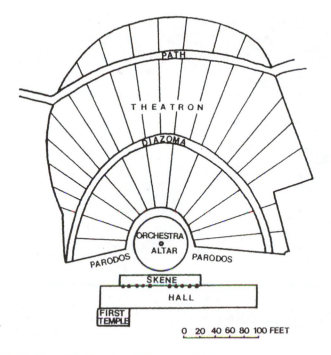

Fig. 1 Plan of the Theatre of Dionysus at Athens.

century BC was the outer surrounding wall. The most important area of the theatre was the circular dancing-floor and acting arena called the *orchestra* which was about 20 metres in diameter and had an altar, *thymele*, at its centre. On either side of the *orchestra* were broad pathways usually referred to as either *eisodoi* or *parodoi*. Not only many of the audience but also the chorus and some of the actors made their entrances and exits by these pathways. Behind the *orchestra* stood the *skene*, at first just a tent in which the actors changed their costumes, but later a wooden building. This wooden building was about 12 metres long and 4 metres high. It had a large central doorway and later possibly a smaller doorway on either side. The roof or upper storey was sometimes used as an acting area: for example, in the opening scene of Aeschylus' *Agamemnon* the Watchman informs us that he is lying 'like a dog' on the roof of the palace; and Dionysus seems to have appeared on the roof for his speech at the end of Euripides' *Bacchae*. Some scholars have suggested that there was a raised platform or stage in front of the *skene* during the fifth century but there is no evidence of this.

Fig. 2 The Theatre, Epidaurus.

The Theatre of Dionysus was rebuilt in stone in the middle of the fourth century BC. Most of the seating became stone benches, offering accommodation for some 15,000 people, but special throne-like chairs were constructed in the front rows for the Priest of Dionysus and other officials. It is difficult to visualise the ancient Athenian Theatre of Dionysus from the site as it is now because of the changes which the Romans made. However, the theatre at Epidaurus, built in the late fourth or early third century BC, is a very well preserved example of an ancient Greek theatre and it gives us an excellent picture of their shape. The bowl-shape of Greek theatres was designed so as to enhance their acoustics. The acoustics at Epidaurus are such that even the smallest sound in the *orchestra* can be heard clearly in the back row; it is unlikely that the Theatre of Dionysus at Athens was quite so perfect in its construction.

The actors

Greek tragedy developed from choral songs on mythological themes. According to tradition, the first actor was a man named Thespis who separated himself from the chorus and acted out the role of a character in the story. The Greek word for actor was *hypocrites*, which literally means 'answerer'. The first actor was referred to as the *protagonistes* (*protos* – first, *agonistes* – competitor or debator). A second actor, the deuteragonist, was introduced at an early stage and by the middle of the fifth century three actors had become standard. All three actors were male. The protagonist usually played only the leading role; the other parts were shared out between the deuteragonist and tritagonist. Silent actors, sometimes referred to as mutes, would be used for attendants and for extra characters such as the non-speaking Pylades in Sophocles' *Electra*. Not only would actors play more than one role within a single play but occasionally the same role might have to be played by different actors during the course of a play. The role of Theseus in Sophocles' *Oedipus at Colonus* provides the best example of this. Rapid changes of costume and mask to transform actors from one character to another took place during the choral odes.

Although three actors were available to tragic poets three-way dialogue rarely occurs. In the whole *Oresteia* trilogy there is only a brief section of the *Eumenides* where Athene, Apollo and Orestes speak one after the other; although three characters are on stage at other points only two of them ever engage in conversation at once. In

Euripides' *Medea*, which was produced much later, only two actors appear in any scene.

Ancient Greek actors needed to be versatile and to have strong voices. At first the playwrights themselves had acted in their own plays but ancient sources record that Sophocles was forced to give up acting early in his career because his voice was too weak. Some roles such as Cassandra in Aeschylus' *Agamemnon* and Antigone in Sophocles'

Fig. 3 Actor from the Pronomos Vase.

Antigone demanded that the actor sang complex lyrics in dialogue with the chorus. The lengthy messenger speeches which occur in so many of the plays also required great stamina and variation in tone. Acting must have been heavily stylised and gestures bold and purposeful. The size of the theatre and the fact that the actors wore masks precluded subtle facial expressions or gestures. Emotions had to be described in the dialogue; there could be no visual clues such as paleness or tears. The grouping of the actors must also have been important for the audience, most of whom would have been looking down on the action from many metres away. The physical positioning of the actors was used to indicate isolation or unity and support.

The chorus

The choral song from which tragedy originated involved a chorus of fifty men. The number of the chorus in tragedies of the fifth century is a much debated topic but it seems likely that either twelve or fifteen were used for each play. Whether the same chorus acted consecutively in all four of a poet's plays is not clear. The importance of the role of the chorus and the proportion of the play given to it seems to have diminished as tragedy developed, although problems of dating some plays and the small number that have survived make it difficult to trace any definite decline. Certainly in the works which we have of Sophocles and Euripides the chorus rarely occupy more than a quarter of the play, whereas in Aeschylus' *Suppliants* the chorus have more than half the lines.

Traditionally the chorus entered the *orchestra* after the prologue and did not leave until the end of the play. The movement from Delphi to Athens in Aeschylus' *Eumenides* provides a notable exception to this rule. Most Greek tragedies are a series of episodes involving the actors, divided by choral odes (to which Aristotle gave the name *stasima*), but there are variations to this pattern: for example, the chorus of Euripides' *Medea* do not have a formal entry ode. The choral odes performed some of the same functions as the curtain does in the modern theatre. They signified the end of a scene, gave an opportunity for the actors to change and sometimes indicated a passage of time. For example, in Sophocles' *Antigone* the Guard departs vowing never to return (331), the chorus sing an ode about the achievements of man, then the Guard returns with Antigone (384). He describes the events since his last appearance and they must clearly have occupied several hours. Some choral odes offer direct comment on the action of the play or fill in the background to events. Others move into an entirely different register and deal with the wonders of gods and men in the manner of a choral hymn, only loosely, if at all, connected to the plot. The playwright could also use his chorus as an interpreter for the audience. In Euripides' *Medea* the chorus are sympathetic initially to Medea and so are we; later they recoil from her crimes and their condemnation of Medea causes the audience to question their own feelings.

As well as singing as a group there are occasions, such as after the murder of Agamemnon in Aeschylus' *Agamemnon*, where the members of the chorus clearly had individual lines. There are also lines within the episodes which are spoken by the chorus and it is generally agreed that these would have been said by the chorus leader.

The chorus did not only sing, they also danced. Little is known for certain about the exact form of these dances, but they seem to have involved large wheeling and circling movements whose patterns would have been easily discernible to the audience above. The arms and body were moved as well as the feet to reflect the emotions appropriate to the song. The musical accompaniment for the tragedies was provided by a flute player (*auletes*) on a sort of double flute with reeds, the *aulos*. He stood in the *orchestra* throughout the performance, wearing long robes but no mask. A lyre was occasionally used to accompany monodies and there was some sort of timpani. We know very little about how the music might have sounded.

Costumes and masks

The Greek actors were covered almost completely by their costumes – a fact which enabled the men more easily to disguise themselves as women and to take on different roles within the same play. The basic garment was an ankle-length robe, called a *chiton*, which by the end of the fifth century invariably had long sleeves. Sometimes a heavier garment, the *himation*, was worn over the *chiton*. At first only the borders of the costumes seem to have been decorated but later the entire robe was richly patterned (see fig. 3). The comic poet Aristophanes makes several jokes about Euripides dressing his heroes in rags but this is probably an exaggeration which should not be taken literally. The chorus' robes were similar to the actors' but were modified so as to be appropriate to their role. For example, the chorus in Aeschylus' *Libation Bearers* wore black robes of mourning as did

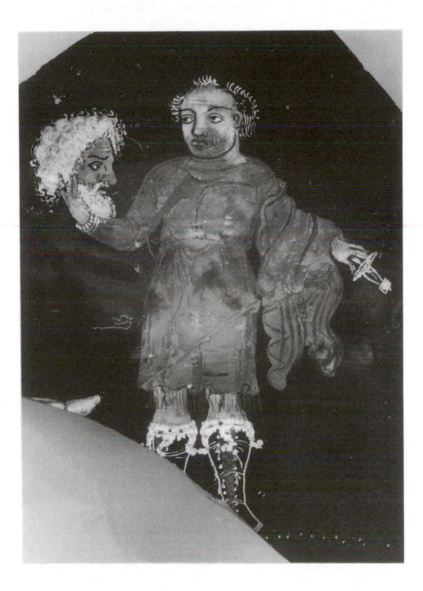

Fig. 4 Actor with mask and buskins, from a late fourth-century vase.

Electra in the same play. The chorus of Aeschylus' *Persae* were undoubtedly dressed as Persians and that of Sophocles' *Philoctetes* as
sailors.

The footwear of tragic actors has been the subject of controversy. A reference in a *Life of Aeschylus* written long after the
poet's death led people to believe that tragic actors wore boots with
platform soles and heels. In fact, such boots were worn in Hellenistic
and Roman times and we have no evidence for their use in the fifth
century. Paintings on pottery show actors both with bare feet and
wearing calf-length boots (see figs 8 & 4). There are references in
fifth-century authors to *kothornoi* – thin-soled soft leather boots
which were loose and fitted either foot; they were commonly worn
by women. Why or how these became the traditional actors' boots,
sometimes referred to as buskins, is uncertain.

The origin of masks (*prosopa*) is equally obscure. Ancient
commentators believed that Thespis first whitened his face with lead
and then decorated it with flowers and that, later, masks of whitened
linen were used. Certainly the masks used in the time of the three
great tragedians covered the whole head and included a luxuriant wig
and a beard, if appropriate (see figs 3 & 4). They were made of linen
or some other base material and then covered in plaster and painted.
Masks were made by specialist craftsmen and the hair and facial
expression would suit the character. A mask for Electra would have
had the close-cropped hair of a woman in mourning, whereas that of
Cadmus in the *Bacchae* would have had grey hair and a beard. In the
Oedipus Tyrannus, Oedipus would obviously have had two masks,
the second showing his bloodied blinded eyes. The high forehead and
wide gaping mouth which are often illustrated belong to the mask of
the Hellenistic rather than the Classical period. It used to be
commonly stated that the mouth of the mask acted as a megaphone
to project the actor's voice throughout the vast auditorium. However,
the excellent acoustics and Sophocles' supposed failure as an actor
because of his weak voice serve to disprove this theory.

Mechanical devices

There were two main mechanical devices used in the ancient Greek
theatre, the *ekkyklema* and the *mechane*. The *ekkyklema* was a
wooden wheeled platform which was brought on and off through the
central doors of the stage building. It was used to display tableaux,
very often the bodies of those murdered off-stage within the house.

The date of its introduction and whether or not it was used by Aeschylus has been the subject of much debate. The *mechane* was a crane; it is sometimes referred to as the *deus ex machina* (god from a machine) because it was primarily used to lift actors playing gods onto the roof of the stage building. Of the tragedians Euripides seems to have used it the most: Medea's dragon chariot at the end of the *Medea* is a good example. Aristophanes used it very frequently in his comedies.

Scene setting

The detailed scene setting contained in the prologues of tragedies, such as Sophocles' *Electra* and *Oedipus at Colonus*, seems to indicate that the audience had to create the scene in their imagination rather than being presented with a realistic representation. However, in his *Poetics* Aristotle credits Sophocles with the introduction of the art of *skenographia*, scene painting. Exactly what form this took, whether it was on a cloth draped over the stage building or on wooden panels placed in front of the building, is not known. In any event, the audience were an enormous distance away from the stage building and could not have seen any subtle details painted on scenery.

There are no indoor scenes in Greek drama and one would not expect to find any. Nonetheless the playwrights seem always to have felt that it was necessary to justify the fact that the action took place out of doors. In Sophocles' *Oedipus Tyrannus* Creon returns from the oracle at Delphi and asks Oedipus whether he should speak in front of everyone or go inside. Naturally Oedipus orders him to speak in front of everyone! In the first scene of Euripides' *Medea* the tutor arrives and asks what the old nurse is doing standing outside the palace talking to herself (delivering the prologue, one is tempted to remark!).

Some stage properties were used. The chariot and crimson cloth in Aeschylus' *Agamemnon*, the urn in Sophocles' *Electra* and the bow in *Philoctetes* were vital symbols and clearly not left to the audience's imagination. Simple items such as swords, crowns and libation jugs would undoubtedly have been commonly used. However, in comparison with the wealth of properties supplied in modern plays to create a realistic atmosphere, Greek tragedies were sparsely furnished.

Special effects were similarly minimal. Some commentators suggest that rocks were used to create a sound of thunder, but whenever thunder occurs it is clearly described in the dialogue and could equally well have been left to the imagination. It also seems unlikely that any attempt was made to portray the collapse of Pentheus' palace in Euripides' *Bacchae* – once again a detailed description is painted in words. There was no stage lighting. Most of the plays which have survived begin at dawn and daybreak is referred to in the prologue. Only the *Rhesus* requires darkness and it is made perfectly plain from the words of the soldiers and from their tripping over one another that the audience must imagine that it is night.

The audience

Apart from the Priest of Dionysus and the magistrates, who else would have been in the audience? Visiting ambassadors definitely attended; women do seem to have been allowed to watch the tragedies but whether large numbers attended is uncertain. Boys went with their slave-tutors. The admission fee was two obols, but the Theoric Fund, introduced by Pericles in the middle of the fifth century, provided money from state funds for all citizens who wished to claim it in order to attend the festival. Each of the ten Athenian tribes was allotted a block of seats; some theatre tickets, small bronze or lead discs, which have survived show a tribe's symbol.

Spectators might take their own cushion, rugs and refreshments. Food and drink were also sold at the theatre. The audiences were more like those at the Elizabethan theatre than the more restrained ones of today. We are told that they hissed, clapped, shouted out remarks and even threw food at the actors. However, from the parodies in Aristophanes' comedies it is also clear that many of the ancient Greek audience had a keen and critical appreciation of the tragedians' techniques. A love of tragedy certainly proved of immense benefit to those Athenians who were captured by the Syracusans after the defeat in Sicily in 413 BC: it is recorded that those who could recite passages from Euripides were released from the tortures of the stone quarries and eventually freed.

Chapter 2
The Drama Festivals

The beginnings of tragedy at the City Dionysia

Tragedy in Athens seems to have developed at the City Dionysia, a festival in honour of Dionysus, god of the vine and fertility. The tyrant Peisistratos, who was not a tyrant in the modern sense of the word but merely a ruler of Athens in the sixth century BC, probably introduced this festival. The City Dionysia, which has also become known as the Great Dionysia, was held at Athens at the beginning of the month Elaphebolion, the equivalent of late March today. At this time the winter was over, the sailing season had begun and visitors came to Athens from all over the known world. By 533 BC a competition in tragedy was a regular part of the City Dionysia. The word *tragodoi* which is used to describe members of the chorus is thought to mean 'goat-singers'. This has led to a variety of suggestions: that the chorus originally wore goat skins, that they competed for a goat, or a goat skin full of wine, or that goat sacrifices were involved. None of these has been satisfactorily proven. The first extant Greek tragedy for which we have documentary evidence is Aeschylus' *Persae* which was produced at the festival in 472 BC.

The arrangements for the competition

The competition between the tragic poets was organised according to strict rules and complicated procedures. (This should not surprise readers who are familiar with the workings of Athenian democracy and the intricacies of matters such as the allocation of jurors to the law courts.) Preparations began a long time in advance of the festival. Would-be competitors had to submit an outline of their intended productions to a magistrate, the archon. The archon had a free choice, although he had to be able to justify his decision to the people. It was clearly easier for an established poet to be selected than an unknown one, but there does not seem to have been any age limit for poets: both Sophocles and Euripides produced plays while in their twenties.

Three tragic poets were chosen to compete and each had to present three tragedies and a satyr play. Aeschylus' *Oresteia* is the only surviving example of a trilogy in which the playwright follows a story through all three plays and presents a resolution of the problem in the third play. Sophocles and Euripides seem to have preferred to present three plays dealing with different stories: for example, in 431 BC Euripides produced the *Medea*, *Philoctetes* and *Dictys*. The three plays of Sophocles about the family of Oedipus which are now commonly presented together as *The Theban Cycle* were in fact produced at widely spaced intervals – *Antigone* in c. 442 BC, *Oedipus Tyrannus* some time after 429 BC and *Oedipus at Colonus* posthumously in 401 BC. It is difficult to generalise about the form of a satyr play, since only one, the *Cyclops* of Euripides, has survived intact, although we do have lengthy extracts from some others. They seem to have been a curious mixture of the tragic and the comic and of the religious and the obscene. They were clearly intended to reduce the tension and powerful emotions engendered by the preceding tragedies. In fact, Euripides offered his *Alcestis*, a tragedy with a 'happy ending', instead of a satyr play at the City Dionysia in 438 BC.

Each playwright was given a *choregos* who acted as a sponsor for his productions. The *choregia* was a liturgy, a kind of supertax on the wealthiest involving payment for things such as the upkeep of a trireme (warship) or a chorus at a festival. These liturgies were often referred to by defendants in lawsuits as proof of their good citizenship. The expense incurred by each *choregos* might be enormous since he had to fund salaries, costumes and the other training costs of a chorus. Some citizens undertook the duty willingly and lavishly, but we also find references to *choregoi* who hired second-hand costumes or to citizens who refused to undertake the duty – permissible if one could find a wealthier man to perform it instead. In times of financial difficulty, such as at the end of the Peloponnesian War, the *choregia* seems to have been shared. Lots were drawn to see which *choregos* would finance the chorus for which poet: for example, in 472 BC the young Pericles was assigned to Aeschylus for his production of the *Persae*.

Poets had originally chosen their own actors; but as the competition became more regulated and special prizes for actors were introduced, the three protagonists were appointed by the state and allocated by lot to the poets. The choice of the other actors seems to have remained in the poets' own hands. The poet was officially called the *didaskalos* (teacher) and he usually trained the chorus himself.

Prior to the festival the *Boule* (a Council of 500 citizens chosen annually by lot) had drawn up a list of those thought suitable to be judges from each of the ten tribes. What their qualifications were expected to be is not known. These names were then placed in ten urns, one for each tribe. The urns were sealed and deposited in the custody of the public treasurers on the Acropolis. Before the contest began, the urns were brought to the theatre and the archon drew out one name from each tribe. The ten judges chosen in this way then had to swear an oath of impartiality. This use of lot-drawing, leaving the decision in the lap of the gods and offering the chance of participation to a large group of people, is typical of the Athenian democracy.

The events of the City Dionysia

The *Proagon* (Preliminary to the Contest) took place on the day before the the statue of Dionysus was taken in a procession to the theatre. It served to publicise the plays in advance of their perform-ance and to rouse enthusiasm and rivalry among the audience. The ceremony took place in Pericles' Odeion from the mid-fifth century. The *choregoi* paraded with their company and each poet in turn mounted a temporarily erected platform and announced the themes of his plays. The actors wore neither costumes or masks for this occasion, but it is possible that they performed excerpts from the plays.

On the following day the statue of Dionysus was escorted in a torchlight procession to the theatre. The statue was carried on a sort of wooden ship on wheels and was accompanied by the *epheboi*, the young men of military age. The statue was present in the theatre for all of the dramatic performances. After this the proceedings moved to the sacred precinct of Dionysus where there was a sacrifice of many animals, including bulls. Other sorts of offerings were also made and these were carried in a procession which included men, women and metics (foreigners with special rights of residence in Athens). The different groups were distinguished, as at the Great Panathenaia in honour of Athene, by the different clothes which they wore and the different gifts which they carried. The metics wore purple robes and carried trays of offerings which were called *skaphia*. The citizens wore ordinary clothes and carried leather bottles, probably filled with wine, on their shoulders; some also carried long thin loaves of bread. A noble-born maiden was chosen to carry a special golden basket containing the first fruits of the Spring. The *choregoi* might dress magnificently for the occasion in rich robes of gold and purple. Once the sacrifices had been made there were choral competitions for men and boys and in the evening there was a *komos*, a revel and an opportunity for uninhibited pleasure. A great deal of wine was drunk and after dark the men took to the streets singing and dancing. They would be accompanied by torch-bearers and musicians playing flutes and lyres.

Representatives of Athens' allies and colonists seem to have been obliged to attend and to present offerings. There was a definite propaganda element in the festival which was used to display the wealth and power of Athens as well as its literary and artistic talent. All public business ceased and the lawcourts were closed for the duration of the festival. Several events of civic importance took place in the theatre before the opening play was performed. Firstly, the names of citizens who had been awarded special crowns for their performance of civic duties were announced. Then the tribute which had been brought by the representatives of the states of the Delian League was displayed in the *orchestra* of the theatre. Finally, the boys whose fathers had been killed in battle and who had been educated at state expense paraded in the theatre. Those who had just reached manhood wore the suit of hoplite armour which the state had provided for them, and a herald proclaimed that they were now independent. Some citizens also seem to have used this time to announce that they were freeing a slave. This ensured a very large number of witnesses to the event, which might prove useful since no state record was kept of the freeing of slaves. The ten *strategoi* (generals), the most important state officials by the middle of the fifth century, attended the festival as a group and offered libations.

During the Peloponnesian War the length of time devoted to the plays was reduced to three days – three tragedies, a satyr play and a comedy being presented each day. Before and after the Peloponnesian War there were four days of plays and five comedies were presented. The proceedings began very early in the morning. The plays each lasted about an hour and there was an interval between them.

At the end of the competition each judge wrote his order of merit on a tablet. These ten tablets were placed in an urn and the archon drew only five of them out. The verdict was decided by the order of merit on these five tablets. The voting was not secret and there are stories of attempts to influence the judges. In the tragedy contest there were originally two prizes, one for the best poet and one for the best *choregos*. A prize for the best tragic actor was introduced in 449 BC. The prizes were traditionally ivy wreathes but there was later a bull for the best poet and a bronze tripod for the winning *choregos*; financial rewards seem to have been introduced at some point as well.

Soon after the festival an Assembly meeting was held at which the conduct of the officials responsible for the arrangements was examined. The archons might be censured or praised. Individual citizens could also use this as an opportunity to complain about other wrongdoings committed during the festival.

Other Athenian drama festivals

The Lenaia was primarily a comedy festival but some tragedy was performed there. It was held at Athens in January in honour of Dionysus. As this was the winter and not the sailing season there were no foreign visitors present. However, metics, the foreigners with special residence rights at Athens, who were often very wealthy, might act as *choregoi* or sing in a chorus at the Lenaia, although they were excluded from doing both at the City Dionysia. Only two tragic poets were chosen to compete and they had to offer two tragedies and no satyr play. Records of this festival go back no further than the middle of the fifth century and at that time both comedies and tragedies were being performed. However, the famous tragic poets of the fifth century rarely seem to have taken part.

Attica was divided into demes, rather like country villages except that families continued to belong to the same deme even if they moved house. Each deme might organise its own Rural Dionysia, usually in December, although the date was not fixed. At some point drama was introduced into these festivals. The best documented example is the festival at the Peiraeus where Socrates is supposed to have gone to see a play by Euripides. There seem to have been troupes of travelling actors who moved from one deme to another. Both comedies and tragedies were performed, but revivals of the popular successes of the great poets were more common than new plays.

Chapter 3
Aeschylus

The poet and his works

Aeschylus, the earliest of the Greek tragedians whose works have survived, was born at Eleusis, some 14 miles from Athens in about 525 BC. He fought against the Persians at the battle of Marathon in 490 BC. Aeschylus won his first victory at a drama festival in 484 BC and he is thought to have written between 73 and 90 plays. The number of his victories is usually given as either 13 or 28; several of his plays were produced again after his death and the larger number may include posthumous victories. Late in his life he visited Sicily and he died there in 456/5 BC. Only six or seven of Aeschylus' plays have survived in anything close to a complete form: *Persae (The Persians)* (472 BC), *Seven Against Thebes* (467 BC), *The Suppliants* (c. 463 BC) *The Oresteia* – a trilogy comprising *Agamemnon, Choephoroi (Libation Bearers)* and *Eumenides* (458 BC) and *Prometheus Bound* (date and authenticity disputed).

The extensive choral odes and the frequent occurrence of lengthy speeches made by a single actor to the chorus in Aeschylean drama reflect its proximity to its choral origins. The poet's language is in many ways similar to that of Homer's *Iliad* and *Odyssey*, rich in compound adjectives, similes and complex imagery. The comic playwright Aristophanes, in his *Frogs* (405 BC), depicted an imaginary contest between Aeschylus and Euripides in the Underworld and parodied the works of both tragedians. Euripides is made to say of Aeschylus:

> ...he would utter a dozen great ox-like words
> with eyebrows and crests, terrible things with monstrous faces,
> unintelligible to the spectators.

(924-6)

Other features which are commented upon in the *Frogs* as being typically Aeschylean are the use of silent characters on stage, the inordinate length of his choral odes and speeches, the militaristic

Fig. 5. Aeschylus.

nature of his dramas and the monotony and repetitiveness of his lyrics. Clearly, Aristophanes' criticisms are exaggerated for comic effect but they would have made little impact unless there was at least an element of truth in them.

Modern critics and commentators have adopted a variety of approaches to Aeschylus' plays. Their poetry, their imagery and symbolism, their visual effects, their portrayal of gods and humans, their connection with contemporary politics and their internal ambiguity and ironies have all been explored and dissected. Moreover, a fierce debate has raged over the authorship of the *Prometheus Bound*; the arguments presented by Taplin and others against its being a genuine work of Aeschylus have persuaded me not to consider it for detailed examination in this chapter.

Apart from the *Persae*, all the extant plays of Aeschylus were written as parts of trilogies on a connected theme. It is fortunate that one of these, the *Oresteia*, has survived virtually intact (part of the prologue of the *Libation Bearers* is missing) so that we may appreciate the scope and subtlety of this form. I shall concentrate upon this trilogy as an example while discussing various aspects of Aeschylus' style, although the middle play, the *Libation Bearers*, will be dealt with in more detail in Chapter 6.

The *Oresteia* was written late in the poet's career and it illustrates a wide range of his techniques. Many critics have noted the considerable differences between the first play, *Agamemnon*, and the last, *Eumenides*: the choral odes take up one-third of the *Agamemnon*, but only one-fifth of the *Eumenides*, although the Chorus have often been regarded as the protagonists of the latter play. Similarly the language of the *Agamemnon* is much more complex than that of the *Eumenides*. In fact, the study of these two rather disparate tragedies written at the same time by the same poet illustrates well the dangers of making sweeping generalisations about the development of 'typically' Aeschylean style.

Language and imagery

The language and imagery of the *Oresteia* has been examined in detail by many scholars, most notably perhaps by Lebeck and Goldhill. Lebeck has rightly pointed out that where there is greatest complexity and ambiguity of language one should not try to find a single correct interpretation but rather admit that Aeschylus intended there to be several possible meanings which his audience might grasp in accordance with their abilities. Much has been written about 'ring-composition' in the *Oresteia*, but one must not forget that the plays were written to be performed and to be experienced in linear fashion by their audience. Recurrent imagery is certainly a feature of the trilogy and an image is often developed more fully as it is repeated; and its full significance may only become apparent later in the trilogy. However, caution must be advised for those studying Aeschylus' use of imagery from English translations. Whenever possible at least two versions should be compared because poetic licence has led translators to extend repeated images, such as those of the net and the hounds, to parts of the text where they do not occur in the original Greek. For example, *Agamemnon* 125 can be literally translated as: '...in time the expedition captures the city of Priam' but Fagles (in his Penguin translation) renders this as: '...years pass and the long hunt nets the city of Priam'.

Aeschylus himself certainly did use imagery associated with nets and traps elsewhere. It first occurs in a choral ode, as a description of Night:

> You who threw your covering net over the towers of Troy
> so that neither the full-grown nor any of the young
> could rise above the great net of all-catching ruin.
>
> (*Agamemnon* 356-60)

Later the Chorus tell Cassandra: 'You are caught inside the nets of fate' (1048) and indeed the trap is closing around the prophetess since Agamemnon had just walked on the crimson cloth and entered the house. Cassandra uses the same imagery in her laments to the Chorus:

> ...what is this appearing? Is it the net of Hades?
> But the net is the woman who shares his bed...
>
> (1114-16)

The reality of the net, as the robe in which Clytemnestra ensnares Agamemnon before she murders him, is foretold in Cassandra's subsequent speech: 'Trapping him in robes she strikes him...' (1126-7). After the murder Clytemnestra herself makes this device explicit:

> So that he might not escape nor avert his fate,
> I surrounded him with a huge encircling net,
> like a fisherman's net, but a deadly richness of robes...
>
> (1380-3)

The Chorus lament the king's death, referring to the 'woven web (*hyphasma*) of the spider' which trapped him (1492 & 1516). Aegisthus uses a similar word when he appears, declaring that Agamemnon lies in 'the woven robes (*hyphantos*) of the Furies' (1580). This makes a double connection: Clytemnestra is seen as an avenging Fury of the household curse and we are prepared for the advent of the Furies themselves later in the trilogy.

The net image occurs several times in the *Libation Bearers* (e.g. 492-3, 506, 980-4, 997-1004 & 1009-15) and Orestes actually displays to the Chorus the net/robe in which his father was murdered after he has killed his mother. The same image is retained in the *Eumenides*, but the nets now belong to the Furies (*Eumenides* 116 & 142) who sing a binding spell to trap Orestes (306ff.). Nets and traps are also used in hunting, another image which pervades the *Oresteia*.

Agamemnon and Menelaus are described as the 'winged hounds of Zeus' (*Agamemnon* 135) in their pursuit of Paris and the Greeks are referred to as 'huntsmen' (695) as they arrive at Troy. The Furies become the hounds and hunters themselves in the *Eumenides* where the image is finally and fully developed (131ff. & 245ff.).

In similar fashion some of the other animal symbolism of the *Agamemnon* develops a greater reality in the subsequent plays. For example, Cassandra refers to Clytemnestra as a snake (*Agamemnon* 1233). In the *Libation Bearers* Orestes describes his mother in the same way (248) and then we hear of Clytemnestra's dream in which she gave birth to a snake (527ff. & 928). At the end of this play the Chorus congratulate Orestes for having 'cut off the heads of two snakes' (1047) but immediately Orestes sees the Furies 'thickly entwined with snakes' (1049-50). The Furies and their snakes are a vital presence in the final play.

Snakes and hounds are not the only beasts which appear in the *Oresteia*. Agamemnon and Menelaus are referred to as eagles on several occasions (e.g. *Agamemnon* 48, 114, 139 and *Libation Bearers* 247 & 258) and lions, bulls and wolves occur at various points. Commentators have also compiled long lists of the legal terminology to be found in the first two plays as preparation for the law court scene in the third. References to sickness and cures and nautical imagery are also widespread. Close study of the text reveals the subtlety with which Aeschylus links images and symbols to one another and to the actual events of the tragedy. The ideas of nets, hunting and beasts are obviously interconnected but one might add to these the recurrent themes of sacrifice and of inescapability and necessity.

The same image is sometimes repeated to describe different circumstances but at the same time forging a link between them. Agamemnon and Menelaus are compared to eagles whose young (i.e. Helen) were stolen (*Agamemnon* 48ff.); but as the choral ode develops the crying for vengeance for lost children seems to be extended to Thyestes' children and to Iphigenia. In the *Libation Bearers* the image is reversed as Orestes calls on Zeus to protect the orphaned nestlings of an eagle (246ff.), which makes a link with the earlier cycle of violence and vengeance. Another example is when the Chorus, referring to Paris, comment:

> Some people deny that the gods think it right
> to ignore a mortal who tramples on
> the beauty of things which are not to be touched.

But he is wicked.

(*Agamemnon* 369-72)

Would the audience have remembered these lines later when Agamemnon agreed to tread on the crimson cloth as he entered the palace? The link must have been intentional even if few were able to appreciate it immediately. Similarly, Orestes, at the beginning of the *Libation Bearers*, sees the Chorus approaching and asks:

What do I see? What is this assembly of women
coming conspicuous in their black clothes?

(10-12)

At the end of the same play he sees other women dressed in black (1049) but these are 'like Gorgons'.

There is also much double speak and irony within the text of the *Oresteia*. The Watchman's speech which forms the prologue of the *Agamemnon* is full of hints about problems within the house. He ends with an elliptical comment:

I speak freely to those who understand,
as for those who do not understand,
my words escape them.

(38-9)

It was part of the tradition of choral lyric that the right words should be said, that words of ill omen should be avoided, and it was believed that words could influence events. For this reason, the Chorus do not describe the actual sacrifice of Iphigenia. Clytemnestra, however, seems to delight in presaging trouble. For example, she comments:

If they respect the gods who hold the city
and the temples of the gods of the captured land
then they, the captors, may not be overthrown in turn.

(338-40)

and

If the army returns without sinning against the gods,
the suffering of the dead may yet be awakened,
if no fresh disaster occurs.

(345-8)

There is a strong idea of willing disaster here and Clytemnestra's hopes are echoed and seem to be fulfilled by the messenger's report: 'Altars have been reduced to nothing and the temples of the gods destroyed...' (527-8). Likewise, the Chorus' remark that: '...the gods do not disregard those who kill many...' (461-2) seems to warn of Agamemnon's impending doom.

Irony and the expression of a wish seem to be combined at the end of Clytemnestra's first speech to Agamemnon:

> Let there be a path spread with crimson cloth
> into the house which he did not expect to see,
> so that Justice may lead him in.
> As for the rest, my care, unconquered by sleep,
> with the gods, will arrange what is fated justly.

> (910-13)

The symbolism of the blood-coloured fabric pouring out of the house is obvious; there is also double meaning in the adjective *aelpton* (which he did not expect) used to describe the house, since the household and the homecoming are not as Agamemnon would have expected them to be. Moreover, Clytemnestra is claiming Justice for herself as she lures Agamemnon to his death. Was there also intended irony in Electra's words which are spoken immediately before Orestes reveals himself in the *Libation Bearers*? Literally translated they are: 'Anguish is present and destruction of one's right mind' (211) – an appropriate description for Orestes at the end of the play! Another, often quoted, example is Clytemnestra's welcome to the disguised Orestes; she offers him a hot bath and a bed (*Libation Bearers* 670-1) – the one the place of Agamemnon's murder, the other of her infidelity. The language of the *Eumenides* is much clearer and more direct and there are few examples of irony or ambiguity within the play.

Subtlety of language can be seen in the choice of individual words within the trilogy: not only do many of them have several shades of relevant meaning but occasionally Aeschylus employs word-play or a pun. The best known is that on the name of Helen, which occurs in the third choral ode of the *Agamemnon*. The Chorus remark that Helen was very aptly named, since the *hel-* part in Greek could be derived from the verb for capturing and killing. They call Helen *helenas, helandros, heleptolis*, that is 'destroyer of ships, destroyer of men and destroyer of cities' (659-60). These adjectives serve to illustrate another point – Aeschylus' fondness, after the manner of Homer, for creating compound adjectives, many of which are not found elsewhere in Greek, by joining together other words. For example, in the first ode of the *Agamemnon* we find *guiobare* (weighing down the limbs), *isopresbys* (like an old man) and *mnesipemon* (reminding one of misery).

Another feature of Aeschylus' writing which is reminiscent of Homer and the epic tradition is his use of 'catalogues'. In the *Agamemnon* there is the detailed description of all the places which made the beacon chain from Troy to Argos. The prologue of the *Eumenides* is a catalogue of the various gods who have held power at Delphi. From the evidence of extant works such lists do not seem to have been so popular with the other tragic playwrights.

Language is clearly a vital ingredient of a tragedy and Aeschylus composed his plays with close attention to the writer's craft. Indeed, some have seen the message of the *Oresteia* as the triumph of language, in the guise of *Peitho* (Persuasion), over *Bia* (Force or Violence).

Spectacle and theatrical effects

Greek tragedy was written to be performed, to be witnessed rather than read. Aeschylus did not just rely on the beauty of his poetry but was eager to create spectacular visual effects for his audience. His ancient biographer, whose accuracy admittedly is open to question, commented that Aeschylus' effects were intended to startle by their strangeness. The same source refers to a tradition that when the Chorus of the *Eumenides* first appeared children fainted and women miscarried. Modern commentators are divided as to exactly which stage equipment would have been available to Aeschylus, but regardless of whether a tableau of bodies was on an *ekkyklema* or not it was still undoubtedly a spectacle.

The stage building was a relatively new feature in 458 BC. The fact that Aeschylus chose to position the Watchman on the palace roof, i.e. on a higher level of the stage building, to deliver the prologue of the *Agamemnon* must have roused the audience's interest and expectation. The next visually dramatic point would have been the arrival of Agamemnon with Cassandra in a chariot. This is swiftly followed by the 'carpet scene'. The 'carpet' was actually a length of rich fabric dyed crimson; it was certainly intended to represent the colour of blood as well as the richness of the house being symbolically poured out. The 'precious things' of the house are being destroyed and the robe in which Clytemnestra entangles her victim is also foreshadowed. The effect of Agamemnon's yielding to Clytemnestra and his removal of his shoes and stepping onto the fabric must have been electrifying. Here was a man visibly committing sacrilege.

Throughout this scene Cassandra remained silent, seated in the chariot; and her descent, after Clytemnestra's departure, provided a new focal point for the spectators.

After the murder of Agamemnon and Cassandra the doors of the stage-building/palace are opened and Clytemnestra, apparently standing over the bodies of her victims, addresses the Chorus. This seems a most suitable tableau for display on the *ekkyklema* although Taplin has argued forcefully against this. The scene is closely paralleled in the *Libation Bearers* when Orestes emerges from the palace, holding aloft the net/robe in which his father had been trapped and displaying the corpses of Clytemnestra and Aegisthus.

The *Eumenides* begins with a prologue by the Priestess of Apollo. Halfway through she begins to enter the temple, only to retreat back to the *orchestra* on all fours (37). It is through her eyes, her reaction and her description that the audience first encounters the Furies. It seems unlikely that the Chorus could have been made to ooze gore realistically or to be as repulsive as their verbal description suggests. Nonetheless, there was a tradition, mentioned previously, that they struck terror in the original audience. Whether they were wheeled out on the *ekkyklema* or whether they entered later, streaming in like a pack of hounds is uncertain. It is not just the Priestess and the Furies who create this atmosphere of terror but also the Ghost of Clytemnestra. Once more, opinions differ; some believe that the Ghost rose from a trap-door in the stage, a rather unlikely explanation since the stage was barely raised, if at all, at this time. Others support the theory that the Ghost was an 'offstage' voice, but such a voice was unlikely to have been heard well and the Ghost has some forty lines to deliver. However, the Athenian audience were used to suspending their disbelief and would not have been unduly perturbed by the fact that an actor portraying a Ghost walked in and out of the *orchestra*.

The Furies leave the *orchestra* in pursuit of Orestes and this departure of the Chorus may have startled the audience. Some commentators have regarded such an exit as unique but Taplin cites parallels in Sophocles' *Ajax*, Euripides' *Alcestis* and *Helen* and in the *Rhesus*. The visual effects of the trial scene are difficult to assess; how far Aeschylus would have moved towards realism is uncertain. I believe that an urn into which the jurors dropped their voting pebbles may have been the only property employed; the idea that a mini courtroom was created is out of keeping with the traditions of tragedy. The *Eumenides* ends with a torchlight procession. Some scholars have imagined an enormous crowd of silent 'extras' here; others have suggested that the entire audience processed out of the theatre (where to and did they come back for the satyr play?), but the effect could equally well have been achieved by those already on stage. Such a procession was a common ending for Attic comedies but seems unusual for a tragedy. Perhaps it symbolised and emphasised the 'happy ending' to the audience.

The gods

Aeschylus' view of Zeus and the other gods has been interpreted in diverse ways. The contrast drawn by Aristophanes in the *Frogs* (885ff.) between the rational Euripides and the traditionally reverent Aeschylus has led many to regard Aeschylus as a champion of traditional religion. In the nineteenth and early twentieth century the popular notion was that Aeschylus had founded a new kind of mono-theism centred on Zeus. This was then countered with a suggestion that Zeus in the plays of Aeschylus is no more developed than the Zeus of Homer. However, a fragment from a lost tragedy, the *Heliades*, has been discovered which reads: 'Zeus is air, Zeus is earth, Zeus is heaven; Zeus is all and whatever is beyond all.' It is not known which character spoke these lines or in what context but they do show that Aeschylus was aware of the possibility that Zeus was something more than the anthropomorphic creation of the epic poets. Some scholars have busied themselves trying to reconcile the dating of various plays with what they see as the 'development' of Aeschylus' conception of Zeus. In the *Suppliants* Zeus is certainly recognised by the Chorus and Danaus as the supreme ruler of the world and he is appealed to frequently, especially in his guises of protector of suppliants and of guests. Yet the Chorus agree that his mind is unfathomable and they are not always confident that he will act with justice (168ff.). The portrait of Zeus as a harsh and vindictive tyrant in the *Prometheus Bound* is one of the reasons that Aeschylus' authorship of the play has been doubted. However, let us return to the *Oresteia*.

(a) Zeus

In their first ode the Chorus of the *Agamemnon* utter the controversial remark: 'Zeus, whatever he may be...' (160) but the rest of the sentence reveals that their uncertainty concerns the appropriate name or cult-title with which to address Zeus rather than doubting his identity or existence:

> Zeus, whatever he may be,
> if it is pleasing to him to be called this,
> I address him in this way.
>
> (160-2)

The Chorus want to be sure that they are using the right words. In this ode they had already spoken of Zeus who sent the sons of Atreus against Paris, calling him the 'mighty protector of guests' (60-2), an epithet repeated several times in the *Agamemnon*. Zeus is also regarded throughout the trilogy as a bringer of justice and vengeance and as one who punishes those who overstep the mark (748, 1022, 1563). He is frequently invoked in this guise by the Chorus, Electra and Orestes in the *Libation Bearers*.

The extent of Zeus' power is illustrated most forcefully in the *Eumenides*. In the prologue the Priestess explains how Zeus gave Apollo his place at Delphi:

> Zeus made his heart inspired with skill
> and placed him as fourth prophet on this throne.
> Apollo is the prophet of his father Zeus.
>
> (17-19)

The Furies too recognise Zeus' power over the other gods when they complain that he ensures that they are treated as outcasts (360f.). However, they also question the morality, or double standards of Zeus: how can he reckon the murder of Agamemnon, a father, to be such a great crime when he had dealt so harshly with his own father, Kronos (640)? The anthropomorphic Zeus of earlier epics and myths momentarily takes the place of the more remote and abstract divine power. A similarly 'human' view of Zeus is revealed by Orestes' first prayer to him in the *Libation Bearers*:

> If you destroy these nestlings of the sacrificer,
> their father, who honoured you greatly,
> from where will you receive a sumptuous offering
> from a hand like his?
>
>
> If you destroy the young of the eagle
> you will not be able to send persuasive signs to mortals,
> nor will this royal family, if wholly withered up,
> support your altars on sacrificial days.
>
> (255-61)

The relationship between men and gods was often seen as a bargain of this kind by the ancient Greeks – men gave gods honour and gods protected men; the benefits were mutual.

Some scholars point out that the Zeus at the beginning of the trilogy is full of vengeance and eager for the destruction of those who oppose him whereas the Zeus of the *Eumenides* acquiesces in the reconciliation of the Furies which is brought about by his daughter Athene. Moreover, in the final play Athene calls Zeus *Agoraios* (973), a title referring to his function especially in public debates. Has Persuasion conquered the Violence in Zeus?

(b) Apollo

Apollo is the only other god who features significantly in all three plays. In the *Agamemnon*, the Chorus recall how Calchas prayed to Apollo to avert Artemis' anger, but the prayer was in vain. Apollo is clearly not able to interfere in Artemis' domain. Calchas had appealed to Apollo the Healer, but another aspect of Apollo is revealed by Cassandra. He had wanted her sexual favours in return for the gift of prophecy. When she refused him he ensured that no one would ever believe her prophecies. In her torment Cassandra rips off the emblems of Apollo which she wears, declaring:

> And now the prophet has finished with me his prophetess
> and has driven me to this deadly fate.
>
> (*Agamemnon* 1275-6)

This is hardly an admirable picture of Apollo.

Orestes makes it very clear in the *Libation Bearers* that he has returned on the specific orders of Apollo to avenge his father's death:

> The mighty oracle of Apollo will not abandon me,
> he ordered me to undergo this danger...
> if I do not pursue those responsible for my father's death...
> he said that I should pay the penalty with my dear life,
> having suffered many miserable disasters...
>
> (269-77)

He goes on to describe the foul spirits from beneath the earth which will pursue him, affected by madness and driven out from his city, if he does not obey Apollo's command. The force of Apollo's oracle is again made clear when Pylades refers to it in the only three lines which he utters in the whole play:

> Where then are the rest of the oracles of Apollo,
> delivered by the Pythian god...?
>
> (900-1)

At this point Orestes has killed Aegisthus but is hesitating to do the same to his mother. After he has murdered her Orestes repeats that he was acting under Apollo's orders (1029-32).

The *Eumenides* opens in the sanctuary at Delphi and we learn from the Priestess how Zeus placed Apollo on its throne. The god himself appears with Orestes, he promises not to give him up but tells him to go to Athens to achieve final absolution. The young man speaks to Apollo almost as if they were equals and reminds him of his duty:

> Lord Apollo, you know what it is not to be unjust;
> since you understand this, learn also not to be neglectful.
> You are capable of acting well and you have the power to do it.
>
> (85-7)

Apollo confronts the Furies at Delphi and begins to argue his case with them. He stresses the importance of marriage, but fails to convince the Furies that killing a husband is a worse crime than killing a mother.

In the trial scene at Athens, Apollo first takes the responsibility for Clytemnestra's murder (*Eumenides* 579), but then he declares that he was merely following the command of his father Zeus. Challenged by the Furies he repeats that it was a far worse crime for the triumphant king to be killed treacherously by his wife. He explains how the mother is not really the parent of a child but merely a storage vessel in which the father's seed develops and he cites Athene, the motherless child of Zeus, as living proof. Apollo promises to make the city of Athens and its people great and to cement an alliance between Athens and Argos (is he trying to bribe the jury?). Critics have ridiculed the weakness of Apollo's arguments and their apparent triviality and irrelevance. It is true that they convince neither the majority of the jurors nor the Furies. But the Furies operate within their own limited parameters just as Apollo does. It is left to Athene to resolve the conflict and Apollo's departure from the court is not even clearly marked.

(c) Athene

Athene, goddess of wisdom and patron of the city of Athens, has not only to decide the issue but to persuade the Furies not to harm the city. She induces them to accept a new, propitious and honourable role in Athens. Athene's part in the *Eumenides* is in some ways similar to a Euripidean *deus ex machina*: she provides a satisfactory conclusion to events and an explanation of how two Athenian institutions, the Areopagus court and the cult of the Eumenides, were established. However, her role is not confined to an epilogue in the Euripidean manner. It is not only Athene's connections with wisdom and Athens which make her especially suitable to be the arbitrator, there is also her position as a female who acts like a male and champions male heroes and so supports Orestes. She is the favoured child of Zeus and is carrying out Zeus' will just as Apollo claims to have done.

(d) The Furies

The Furies (*Erinyes*) are not Olympians, they belong to the older chthonic gods. Their presence is felt from the opening chorus of the *Agamemnon* in which the old men sing of the Furies, represented here by the sons of Atreus, sent against Troy by Zeus. Each time the Furies are mentioned in the *Agamemnon* they are avenging spirits, often acting at the bidding of Zeus. They are not necessarily avenging bloodshed within a family but rather they punish any sin against the divinely appointed code. The Chorus of the *Agamemnon* equate Helen with a Fury sent to bring retribution on Troy (748). Once Clytemnestra has lured Agamemnon into the palace, the Chorus sing of a Fury which is filling them with dread (991ff.) and accuse Cassandra of conjuring up Furies as she describes her visions to them (1119). The prophetess herself later claims to see the Furies connected with the curse of Atreus clustering around the palace (1190). These Furies are the avengers of bloodshed and it is to them that Clytemnestra claims that she has sacrificed Agamemnon (1433).

The Furies are first mentioned in the *Libation Bearers* by Orestes, who somewhat ironically is concerned that he will be pursued by these foul monsters if he does *not* murder Clytemnestra. Orestes is also aware of the Fury of the house of Atreus and he tells Electra:

> The Fury has not been starved of murder
> and now it will drink undiluted blood
> for the third time.
>
> (577-8)

Curiously Clytemnestra had also claimed to have provided the third draught for the Fury (*Agamemnon* 1476), but perhaps Orestes has discounted Iphigenia. At the end of the *Libation Bearers* the Furies become a reality for Orestes:

> ...women like Gorgons dressed in black
> and entwined thickly with snakes...
> These are not the fancies of my torments,
> these are clearly the malignant hounds of my mother...
> they are dripping blood from their eyes...
>
> (1048-58)

Clytemnestra had threatened him with hounds such as these before she was killed (912 & 924).

In the *Eumenides* this vision has indeed become reality as the Furies take their place as the Chorus. They are whipped into action by the Ghost of Clytemnestra. Their aim is a simple one, to hunt down the matricide and to exact blood and pain in return for a mother's blood. They believe that the shedding of a relative's blood is a far more heinous sin than the murder of a mere connection by marriage. Their sphere of action seems much narrower than in the earlier parts of the trilogy. After their defeat at the trial they are persuaded to become the Eumenides, the Kindly Ones, (although this name does not appear anywhere in the Greek text of the entire *Oresteia*) and to make their home at Athens where they will bless the crops and protect the citizens from civil war.

Much has been written about the conflict between the old and the new gods in the *Oresteia*. Some scholars have seen the trilogy as an allegory of the shift from the ancient matriarchal society and its vendetta code of 'an eye for an eye' to the patriarchal democracy with its rule of law and predominantly male (or male disposed) Olympian gods. This theory is highly speculative and assumes both that there was such an evolutionary development and that Aeschylus was conscious of its having occurred. The Olympians are in place long before the trilogy's dramatic starting point and the idea of a blood feud or vendetta was still current in fifth-century Athens – for example, the curse of the Alcmaeonids was invoked against Pericles by his enemies. The Furies may have been reconciled at the end of the *Oresteia* but they do not cease to exist.

Human characters

It is a matter of debate whether Aeschylus merely presented his audience with 'types' whose behaviour and speech were dictated by the needs of the plot or whether he attempted to portray 'real' people with human feelings and psychological motivation. Critics usually cite Aristotle's *Poetics* (1450a & 1454a) where he states that 'character' should be subordinate to plot in tragedy. However, the Greek word translated as 'character' is *ethos* which literally means 'attitude' or 'disposition' rather than 'character' in the modern sense of the word. The most extreme suggestion is that Aeschylus made no attempt to create consistent characters but wrote whatever was appropriate to each particular scene without reference to any other. One problem is that characters in Aeschylus' tragedies rarely engage in conversation; they tend rather to address the chorus or make long general pronouncements. In the *Agamemnon* the only real exchange between two characters is the short debate between the King and his wife before he walks on the crimson fabric. Another problem is that of 'free will': many commentators have regarded the human characters in Aeschylus' plays, and in the *Oresteia* in particular, merely as puppets of the gods rather than as humans acting of their own accord.

(a) Clytemnestra

The only character who appears in all three plays is Clytemnestra and she is also the most dominant of the humans. Is she merely a 'type' or are there any signs that Aeschylus has consciously endeavoured to create an individual personality for her? The first reference to Clytemnestra in the trilogy is made by the Watchman in his prologue: 'For so a woman's hopeful, manly-planning heart exercises its power...'(*Agamemnon* 10-11). This picture is reinforced at Clytemnestra's first meeting with the Chorus. She is determined to be taken seriously and she will not tolerate criticism. After her description of the course of the beacon message and the possible scene at Troy, the Chorus comment: 'Woman, you speak with good sense, like a wise man' (351). Agamemnon himself remarks that Clytemnesta's behaviour is not that of a woman (940) when she persists in her efforts to persuade him to walk on the crimson cloth.

Clytemnestra's strength and masculinity are further highlighted in the final scene of the *Agamemnon* where they are contrasted with the weakness of her lover Aegisthus. Aegisthus appears only briefly in the first two plays; his role in the saga was well known and could not be omitted from the drama, but in Aeschylus' version his main purpose seems to be to act as a foil to Clytemnestra. He enters after she has claimed full responsibility for the murders and reminds the Chorus how his father Thyestes had been abused by Agamemnon's father Atreus. He then claims that he was responsible for the King's death. The audience's view of Aegisthus would have already been coloured by the words of Cassandra who had described him as a 'strengthless lion' (1224) and as a wolf who slept with a lioness (1258). The Chorus' reaction to Aegisthus and their blatant lack of respect for him only reinforce this impression. The frail old men of the Chorus taunt him and address him as 'woman' (1625). They almost come to blows with Aegisthus and his bodyguard but for the intervention of the powerful Clytemnestra who commands them not to fight. They obey her.

In the *Agamemnon*, Aeschylus was clearly attempting to create the idea of a strong, powerful and masculine personality for Clytemnestra. How far is this projected by her actual speech and actions and what other sorts of emotions and characteristics, if any, does she show? She is totally confident in her dealings with the Chorus as she describes in detail the beacon chain. Her reaction to the Herald is arrogant and she dismisses him with a totally false message to her husband:

> When he comes into his house let him find
> as faithful a woman as he left behind,
> a noble guard dog of the house for him,
> hostile to those who are his enemies
> and the same in all other respects,
> not having broken the seal on his property in this length of time.
> Not from any other man, have I known pleasure
> nor speech causing scandal,
> any more than I know about the tempering of bronze.
>
> (606-12)

This speech may well have shocked the audience with its patent lies. Interestingly, the Herald does not leave at once as he was commanded but stays to report the fate of Menelaus to the Chorus; he is one man who is not intimidated by Clytemnestra!

The Queen's speech of welcome to Agamemnon is similarly full of blatant falsehood. She claims to have attempted suicide several times, distraught at reports of Agamemnon's death and to have sent Orestes away because of danger from the people of the city. There follows the debate over the crimson cloth. This is probably the most discussed section of the entire trilogy: it has been seen as a contest of arguments resembling those of a rhetorical handbook, as a deeply psychological battle of wills and as a further demonstration of Clytemnestra's manipulative power. Agamemnon initially refuses to trample on the cloth because he fears the envy of the gods, but the Queen challenges him that he might have vowed just such an action to the gods in a moment of fear and would then have carried it out without compunction. She next points out that if Priam had been the victor at Troy he would not have hesitated to walk on rich fabrics; will Agamemnon fear to do the same? Agamemnon refers to the danger of exciting public disapproval, but Clytemnestra retorts that envy goes hand in hand with admiration. Finally, Agamemnon yields; he removes his shoes and prays that no god's anger may strike him for spoiling such rich treasures. Clytemnestra, triumphant, calls on Zeus to accomplish her prayers. Agamemnon entered the scene as a victor, but he leaves defeated, Clytemnestra once more has the upper hand. In one sense her victory is short-lived; she turns to Cassandra and orders her to enter the palace, but the prophetess completely ignores the Queen's commands.

Once Clytemnestra has left the stage Cassandra begins to speak, creating a vivid picture of the Queen as a monster. She refers to her as a 'hateful bitch' (1227), 'a double headed serpent' and a 'Scylla' (a six-headed monster) (1233). Clytemnestra's gloating after she has committed the murders and her obvious delight in being splashed with blood confirm this view of her as a monster. She also claims to have derived special pleasure from killing Cassandra, her husband's mistress whom she says was used to lying on her back on the rowing benches (1442). Some scholars have interpreted this not just as sexual jealousy but also envy of those women who were involved with the men and the fighting at Troy while she was left at home. This seems to be a rather extreme interpretation, but so does its opposite, propounded by Rosenmeyer, that Clytemnestra was devoid of all feeling, had no passion for Aegisthus nor anger because of the death of Iphigenia but merely regarded the latter impersonally as the latest manifestation of the ancestral curse.

However, once the Chorus have mentioned the curse on the house of Tantalus (1468f.) Clytemnestra shifts her ground and refers to herself as the avenger of Atreus (1500f.). Does Aeschylus intend us to see the curse of the House as the driving force behind the action and Clytemnestra as its tool or is the queen using the curse as a pretext for her own ends? Some critics have seen parallels between Clytemnestra and Athene: both are noted for their manly characteristics and their ability to fulfil a 'man's role', both are able to win over others by the force of persuasion – but Clytemnestra's masculinity leads to disaster while Athene's leads to success. The Chorus repeatedly refer to the destructive influence of Helen, the sister of Clytemnestra. They also name her as an avenging Fury, a role which the Queen claims for herself at the end of the play. Surely at least some members of the audience would have made a connection between the disreputable, man-destroying Helen and her sister?

In the *Libation Bearers* Clytemnestra's role is less dominant and she seems to be less confident and powerful. She is spoken of with bitterness by Electra in her opening exchanges with the Chorus and in later ones with Orestes, for example:

> My mother, in no way an appropriate name,
> since she has acquired an ungodly heart towards her children...
>
> (190-1)

The Chorus stir up further resentment against Clytemnestra by recalling how she mutilated Agamemnon (439). They also give Electra and Orestes fresh hope when they explain the Queen's dream about the snake, saying that she is 'quivering with fear' (524) and 'terrified' (535). This does not seem consonant with the bold and shameless queen of the first play. When Clytemnestra herself appears and greets the disguised Orestes she seems nothing more than a polite hostess, but the final lines of her speech of welcome fit oddly with her *androboulos* (planning like a man) image in the previous play:

> If it is necessary to deal with something else,
> more a matter for planning, this is the work of men,
> to whom we shall communicate it.
>
> (672-3)

On hearing of Orestes' 'death' Clytemnestra reacts with grief and claims that she has been 'destroyed'. Whether this reaction was intended to be genuine and spontaneous or hypocritical is hard to tell. Cilissa, Orestes' old nurse, later reports to the Chorus that the queen was covering up her happiness with a sad expression (738).

In contrast to her previous demeanour, as soon as Clytemnestra discovers that Orestes is alive and that he has killed Aegisthus she shouts for a 'man-slaying axe' (889). Confronted by her son she pleads with him and displays the breast which suckled him (896f.). This reminds us of the dream in which she suckled a snake who drank her blood, but the image is also undermined by Cilissa's earlier speech in which she had recalled how she, not his mother, had been the wet nurse of Orestes. As her persuasion fails, Clytemnestra resorts to threats and twice warns of the mother's curse which will hound Orestes (912 & 924) – a preparation for the appearance of the Furies. Clytemnestra is assuredly not the boastful victor in the *Libation Bearers* which she was in the *Agamemnon*.

Her part in the *Eumenides* is slight; her ghost is mainly a device for introducing the arguments of the Furies and for rousing them to action. However, it is also noteworthy that her ghost feels mocked and dishonoured – a far cry from the confident Clytemnestra of the first play. Does this lend credence to those who argue that Aeschylus was not interested in creating consistent characters? It seems to me that in the first play Aeschylus has used the speeches of other characters to create an impression of Clytemnestra as something more than a mere 'type'. How successfully this is transferred to Clytemnestra's own actions and her character in the rest of the trilogy is the nub of a scholarly controversy; readers will reach their own conclusions.

(b) Agamemnon

Agamemnon, as mentioned earlier, yields to Clytemnestra's persuasion and falls into her trap. Critics have suggested all sorts of reasons for his capitulation – he was an arrogant man and was flattered by such honour, he was too tired after the war to do battle with his wife (there is much battle vocabulary used during the exchange), or he was an old-fashioned gentleman who deferred to his wife out of politeness. Others have simply cited the dramatic necessity for him to tread on the fabric, apparently commit *hubris* (a sin of pride against the gods) and enter the house where he will be murdered.

Although Agamemnon only speaks some 82 lines in the trilogy his presence is felt throughout. The Watchman and Clytemnestra are waiting for news of his return; the Chorus sing of his expedition as divine avenger to Troy and of his sacrifice of Iphigenia in their first ode. In their second ode they refer to the anger of the citizens against the sons of Atreus because of the

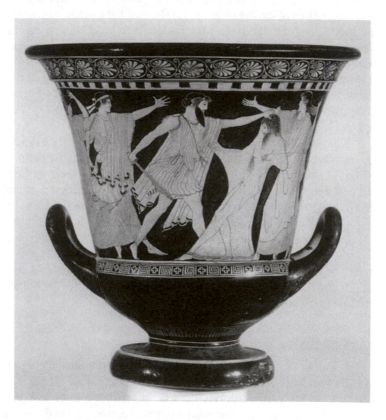

Fig. 6 The murder of Agamemnon, from a fifth-century red-figure vase.

deaths caused by their expedition for the sake of one woman. They admit these feelings to Agamemnon himself on his return (*Agamemnon* 799ff.) but add that they are now sincerely pleased to see him. Agamemnon's speech in reply is a set piece, devoid of any emotions: he thanks the gods for his victory, comments on men's loyalty, plans a council to sort out any problems in the state and prepares to enter the palace to make sacrifice to the gods. After the debate with Clytemnestra he treads on the fabric and goes to his death. Cassandra also provides a powerful contrast to Agamemnon. The King returns home as victor, she comes as a slave to a foreign land;

he is defeated by Clytemnestra and enters the palace under her control, Cassandra refuses to yield to the Queen and enters in her own time; he enters the palace deceived and in ignorance, whereas she enters with full knowledge of what is to come.

One sympathises with those who see Agamemnon as a cipher, a stock victorious general who has no personality of his own. However, as soon as he has been killed all complaints about his responsibility for numerous deaths in the Trojan War and the sacrifice of Iphigenia are forgotten by the Chorus. He was their king and was murdered dishonourably and they long for Orestes to return and take vengeance. This theme is sustained throughout the *Libation Bearers*, even though the Chorus there are women enslaved by this same king. In the trial scene of the *Eumenides* Apollo describes Agamemnon as 'a noble man, honoured with a god-given sceptre' and 'a man respected by everyone' (625-6). Agamemnon has taken his place as the hero of the legend.

(c) Free will and suffering

However well or sketchily drawn one concludes that the characters of Aeschylus are, there remains the controversy over 'free will'. Distinguished scholars have lined up in support of both sides of the argument. Some believe that Agamemnon had a choice as to whether to sacrifice Iphigenia at Aulis and that the poet indicated this when he wrote: ' . . . he put on the harness (yoke strap) of necessity' (*Agamemnon* 218). After this, they argue, Agamemnon was doomed and his delusion made him unable to resist Clytemnestra's persuasion. They see moments of choice too at Cassandra's entry to the palace, when Orestes hesitates to kill his mother and when the Furies are reluctant to accept Athene's offer. On the other side, scholars point to the repeated assertions that everything which happened was the will of Zeus and was fated and they stress that the yoke which Agamemnon put on was 'of necessity' and he therefore had no choice. Likewise, did Orestes really have a choice when he was threatened with his father's furies by Apollo? Are the human characters mere puppets of divine will as the household curse is worked out?

In the *Agamemnon* the Chorus comment that Zeus decreed that only those who suffer learn (177). Do any of the human characters gain wisdom? Agamemnon does not seem to have learnt anything before he is killed, nor does Aegisthus. Clytemnestra gains a little insight after her murder of Agamemnon and Cassandra when she realises that she may be an instrument of the curse and she wishes vainly that she may have put an end to that curse (*Agamemnon* 1567f.). Orestes is fully conscious of the enormity of his crime before he commits it, but not of its consequences. He is unable to resist divine will or the pressure to fulfil his duty. Perhaps the only characters who suffer and then learn in the trilogy are not humans at all – but the Furies.

The role of the chorus

The huge proportion of the trilogy taken up by choral odes was noted at the beginning of this chapter. These odes are typically concerned with prayer, lament or thanksgiving. The chorus function as a narrator and as an enunciator of wisdom, they create a mood, remind the audience of past events and prepare them for actions to come. In Aeschylus' plays the chorus also receive the speeches of the main characters and engage in discourse with them. Some commentators assert that the chorus invariably represent the poet's own views and values but this assumes a unity and consistency in their statements which are not always present.

The Chorus of the *Agamemnon* consists of men who were too old to set out with the expedition to Troy (some ten years earlier) and their age and frailty is mentioned at several points, for example:

> We, without honour because of our old flesh,
> were left behind then from the military expedition.
> We stay here supporting our childlike strength
> on our sticks...

$$(72\text{-}3)$$

Their first ode of some 223 lines tells of the expedition against Troy and the sacrifice of Iphigenia and they pray that good fortune is to come. Each successive ode is shorter than the last. They are respectful towards Clytemnestra although they initially doubt her claim that Troy has fallen. After her explanation of the beacon chain they sing of the fall of Troy, but the song changes to one of the horrors of war and the unrest caused in the city by the expedition. It is the Chorus not Clytemnestra who extract information from the Herald about the Greeks' victory and they sing another ode about Helen and Troy before Agamemnon himself arrives. Here they seem (to be fulfilling the traditional function of covering a passage of time, although some modern critics dispute that there was any notion of the need to account for time logically in Greek drama.

As in the case of the Herald, it is the Chorus who greet Agamemnon first and they hint that all may not be well in the city. Once Agamemnon has entered the palace, after a brief ode of foreboding and loss of hope, the Chorus seem almost to exchange roles with Cassandra. It is she who now sings of the history of the house and its curse, who warns of disaster to come and who creates an atmosphere of tension and doom. The Chorus are unable to understand her allusions or grasp her meaning until she finally departs. When they hear Agamemnon's death cries from within the palace the Chorus dissolve into disorder and speak severally, so mirroring the disruption of the natural order as the King is murdered by his wife. Their lack of action and dithering has been the butt of much parody but it reflects the genuinely confused reaction of ordinary people. They are shocked by Clytemnestra's open boasting over her victims but they do not attempt to oppose her. It is only the 'womanish' Aegisthus and his threats which finally rouse them so that they are prepared to fight.

The main function of the Chorus of slave women in the *Libation Bearers* is to support Electra and Orestes. They advise Electra as to how to carry out the sacrifice at her father's tomb and then join with her and Orestes in a lengthy invocation of the spirits of the dead, appealing for aid in avenging Agamemnon. The Chorus are also able to reveal Clytemnestra's dream about the snake, which Orestes accepts as a favourable omen. However, their most remarkable intervention and one quite out of keeping with the often neutral role of a chorus, is their instruction to Cilissa to tell Aegisthus to come unarmed. They make this request entirely on their own initiative and in doing so give Orestes invaluable assistance.

In the final play of the trilogy Aeschylus chose the Furies themselves as the Chorus and virtually the protagonists of his drama. Their language changes as they are transformed from the bloodthirsty hounds of hell to the guardians of Athenian prosperity. Reconciled they are finally led off in triumphant procession like the revellers of Old Comedy. Without doubt the Chorus was indispensable to the *Oresteia*.

Political and social comment

Some scholars assert that Greek tragic playwrights were motivated to a large extent by a desire to promote their views on contemporary issues; others deny the existence of any specific reference to a contemporary event or person in extant Greek tragedy. Taplin, for example, supports the latter view, discounting Aeschylus' *Persae* on the grounds that it is about Persians not Athenians and that they are treated like heroes from the legendary past. I suspect that the truth lies somewhere between the two extremes. Athenian playwrights were closely involved in the social and political life of their city and it would be strange if their writings were totally devoid of the influence of current affairs or allusions to contemporary issues. After all, Aristophanes did claim in the *Frogs* that a playwright's duty was to teach citizens and he did make Dionysus ask Aeschylus and Euripides for advice about Alcibiades and other problems of the city.

The *Oresteia* has provoked an enormous number of theories about its political significance and symbolism. It was produced some three years after the major democratic reform instigated by Ephialtes and others by which the old, aristocratic Areopagus Council was stripped of most of its powers. Its main function was now to act as a court in certain murder cases while its political powers had been distributed between the democratic Council (*boule*) and the People's Assembly (*ekklesia*). It has been suggested that Aeschylus wrote the *Oresteia* to placate the aristocrats by reminding them of the divine origins of the Areopagus as a court for murder trials, or as a celebration of the radicals' victory, or as an attempt at peace-making between the two parties. Others connect the plays with the recent murder of Ephialtes and see them as an appeal for harmony and an end to bloodshed and retaliation. However, the date and circumstances of Ephialtes' death are disputed by historians.

Three references to the alliance made between Athens and Argos in the winter of 460/1 have been noted in the *Eumenides* (288-91, 667-72 & 762-7). Traditionally Agamemnon had been king of Mycenae not Argos, although by the fifth century BC Argos was the ruling city of the whole area. Some commentators believe that Aeschylus deliberately altered Mycenae to Argos in his trilogy in order to extol the virtues of the alliance of Argos and Athens against Sparta. A more extreme suggestion is that Aeschylus was using the curse of the family of Tantalus as a mythical prototype for the curse of Cylon on the Athenian Alcmaeonid family. The aristocratic Alcmaeonids were under attack from their political opponents at this time and may well have supported the idea that curses could be ended, but any link between them and the composition of the *Oresteia* can only be a very tenuous one. Several other references in the *Eumenides* have been linked with contemporary Athenian campaigns (e.g. 398 with Sigeum). Whether such references were intentional is difficult to assess. It is true that the works of Aeschylus have layers of meaning but it seems wantonly destructive to reduce them simply to the level of political allegory, especially when the precise historical facts themselves are at best only partially known.

A more striking and interesting aspect, but one which is rarely commented upon, is the attitude shown to war in the *Oresteia*. Aeschylus was caricatured by Aristophanes as the supporter of the traditional martial hero and his role in the battle of Marathon against the Persians is universally recognised. Indeed, it was this rather than his tragedies which was mentioned in his epitaph. Moreover, it is Euripides who is often labelled the anti-war poet. However, at several points in the *Agamemnon* there are powerful descriptions of the grim and inglorious realities of war. In their first ode the Chorus comment:

> ...causing many struggles
> weighing down the limbs for both Greeks and Trojans,
> their knees pressed down in the dust,
> spear shafts being shattered in the first onslaught.
>
> (63-7)

Clytemnestra also paints a vivid picture as she imagines the scene on the night that Troy was captured:

> ...they have collapsed
> around the corpses of their menfolk, their brothers,
> and children fall on the bodies of aged parents,
> they lament the fate of their loved ones
> with a voice which is no longer free...
>
> (326-9)

She then describes how the Greeks will be able to sleep for the first time in houses away from the frosts and dampness of the night. This shows clear awareness of the discomforts of camp life.

In their second ode the Chorus describe the misery felt at home when ashes were returned in place of men:

> ...instead of men, urns and ashes come into each house.
> Ares, the money-changer of bodies, holds his scales in the battle
> of spears,
> from the fire at Troy he sends to loved ones dust
> heavily laden with bitter tears,
> packing urns, easy to fill, with ashes in place of men.
>
> (434-44)

Most significantly, the Herald, who had actually been at Troy, describes what it was like:

> If I were to speak of the hard work,
> the uncomfortable sleeping quarters,
> the narrow decks of the ships and the terrible resting-places...
> what did we not groan about, what did not fall to our daily lot?
> Then again, on dry land there was even more discomfort,
> for our beds were by the walls of the enemy
> and the meadow dew continually dropped on us
> from the sky above or rose from the ground below,
> bringing ruin to our clothing and lice to our hair.
> And if anyone were to speak of the winter,
> which kills all the birds
> and which sends unendurable snow to Mount Ida,
> or the heat of the summer...

(555-65)

A single theme emerges from these extracts – war brings little joy to anyone. Some might suggest that Aeschylus included these descriptions to remove the glamour from the conquering hero Agamemnon and to prepare for his death. Others might see a link with the war against the Peloponnesians which was just beginning. Was Aeschylus speaking out against war or showing the audience, most of whom would have fought for their country, that he understood what they endured as soldiers? Whatever the motive, these passages certainly indicate that Aeschylus was aware of the horrors of war and their effect on ordinary men and women. He clearly does not glorify war for its own sake.

Conclusion

As we have seen, Aeschylus was undoubtedly a master of his craft and this is well illustrated by the *Oresteia*. Recurrent images are woven into the trilogy and themes and symbols are repeated. There are other more fundamental connections between the plays of the trilogy. The parallels between the plots of the *Agamemnon* and the *Libation Bearers* are quite remarkable. In the *Agamemnon's* first scene the questions are posed 'Has Troy fallen, is the evidence to be trusted?'; in the *Libation Bearers* 'Has Orestes returned, is the evidence to be trusted?' In each play the murder is preceded by a confrontation and debate between murderer and victim. After the murders in both plays we are shown a tableau of bodies, in each case a man and a woman who were lovers. In the first a man returns home openly and is killed by a woman; in the second a man returns home secretly and kills a woman. In the *Agamemnon* a father has killed a daughter, in the *Libation Bearers* a son kills a mother. In both plays a long awaited return ends in disaster.

Within the trilogy Aeschylus explored the relations of humans to the gods, the complex problems within a family, the true meaning of justice and its link with the city. The suffering of the first two plays is diminished in the third as the trilogy moves towards resolution and reconciliation, the climax coming not with the acquittal of Orestes but with the conversion of the Furies.

After his death Aeschylus' talent was recognised with an unusual honour: his plays were allowed to be performed at the major drama festivals in competition with the newly-written works of other poets. Clearly, the Athenians believed that there was much to be gained from a second viewing of his plays.

Chapter 4
Sophocles

The poet and his works

Sophocles (496-c. 406 BC) had a career which spanned more than sixty years, overlapping both Aeschylus and Euripides. He participated in his first tragic competition in 468 BC and his last tragedy, *Oedipus at Colonus*, was produced posthumously in 401 BC. Only 7 of his estimated 123 plays are now extant and few of these can be accurately dated: *Ajax* (c. 447 BC), *Antigone* (c. 442 BC), *Trachiniae* (?438-2 BC), *Oedipus Tyrannus* (after 429 BC), *Electra* (?420-10 BC), *Philoctetes* (409 BC) and *Oedipus at Colonus* (401 BC).

Sophocles has been described as the greatest innovator of the Greek tragedians. This reputation can be traced to the *Poetics* of Aristotle who stated that 'Sophocles introduced three actors and scenery painting'. Another ancient source suggested that Sophocles was also responsible for the introduction of three single plays instead of the connected trilogy, but this is refuted by evidence that Aeschylus produced three unconnected plays in 472 BC, before Sophocles had even entered a contest. In fact, signs of startling departures from tradition in the surviving works of Sophocles are scarce and Aristophanes in his *Frogs* portrayed Euripides not Sophocles as the revolutionary or radical playwright. There are obvious dangers and difficulties in generalising from such a limited number of plays, but at the same time one can only work from the evidence which has survived. The tragedies of Sophocles have certainly been the focus of much modern scholarship. Particular themes seem to be dominant: characterisation, the Sophoclean tragic hero, the role of his chorus, the relationship of his gods to men, his language and use of irony.

In this chapter I shall examine the *Antigone* and the *Oedipus Tyrannus* in detail, focusing on some of these themes and suggesting other lines of approach. The *Electra* will be discussed in Chapter 6. The *Antigone* has been described as a play dealing with conflicts, such as those of divine law and man-made law, family and state, female and male, but to reduce it to such stark antitheses is to ignore the complex

Fig. 7 Sophocles.

subtlety of Sophocles' skill as a playwright. At the other end of the spectrum Goldhill has written a masterly exposition on the use of the words *philos* (friend, relative) and *ekhthros* (enemy) in the *Antigone*, but such detailed study is beyond the scope of this book. Aristotle regarded *Oedipus Tyrannus* as one of the best examples of Greek tragedy because it involved a simultaneous *peripeteia* (reversal or change of circumstances) and *anagnorisis* (recognition or discovery), and evoked both pity and fear from the audience. The Oedipus legend was well-known to the people of Athens and had already been dealt with in a trilogy produced by Aeschylus in 467 BC. Sophocles' plot concentrates not upon an action, but upon the revelation of actions which have already occurred and gives much scope for the use of irony.

Characterisation and the Sophoclean tragic hero

Skilful portrayal of character has been regarded as a Sophoclean hall-mark since ancient times, but as Goldhill has rightly pointed out the Greek word *ethos,* which is used in both the *Life of Sophocles* and by Plutarch, does not really correspond to our modern term 'character'. The famous German scholar, Tycho von Wilamowitz-Moellendorff, in a controversial thesis published early this century, adopted Aristotle's view that plot took precedence over character and argued that Sophocles did not aim to create convincing characters and sometimes did not even bother to ensure that his characters were consistent. Other more recent scholars have re-asserted the view that Sophocles was interested in depicting people as individuals and building up a personality for them. Sophocles' treatment of the tragic hero has been much discussed and a common conclusion is that his human characters, unlike those of Aeschylus, stand apart from the gods, 'naked and defenceless' and that they have to learn for themselves humility and the limits of man's situation.

There has been intense debate as to whether Antigone or Creon is the 'tragic hero' of the *Antigone*; but it has now been recognised that the idea that a tragedy should deal with the reversal of fortune of a single figure is based on a misreading of Aristotle. There is no reason why the characters Antigone and Creon should not be given equal weight, nor should one ignore the others, Haemon, Eurydice and Ismene, who are drawn inexorably into the disaster.

(a) Antigone

Sophocles used a series of confrontations to illuminate the thoughts, motives and temper of Antigone and Creon. In the opening scene Ismene acts as a foil to her impassioned and determined sister. Antigone adopts a defiant attitude from the outset and claims that Creon has made the edict specifically against her:

> Creon has made this proclamation for you and me,
> indeed for me, I say...

> (*Antigone* 31-2)

an idea which is later contradicted by Creon's reaction to the news of the burial. Ismene speaks as a representative of reason and obedience to the law, sympathetic but unwilling to sacrifice her life pointlessly, as she sees it:

...we must reflect upon this,
firstly that we are women, not meant to fight against men
and then that we are ruled by those much stronger
and we must obey...
to take extreme action is not at all sensible.

                                                        (61-8)

The theme of Antigone's lack of *nous* (sense) is one which recurs throughout the play and Antigone's response to her sister's mild advice clearly denotes her as an extremist. She, Antigone, will act alone and will die for her belief, 'having committed a holy crime'; whereas Ismene does not want to dishonour the gods, but she sees herself as powerless.

Antigone carries out her plan and is arrested on her second visit to the body and brought to Creon. She is uncompromising and asserts:

It was not Zeus who made this proclamation,
nor did that Justice which lives with the gods below
lay down such laws for men.
Nor did I think that your edicts were so strong
that you being a mortal were able to override
the unwritten, everlasting laws of the gods.

                                                        (450-5)

This is the crux of Antigone's argument – the gods declare that all men should have funeral rites, an idea found in Homer, *Odyssey* XI, 73, and in many other sources. It is her duty as next of kin to ensure that these rites are carried out and she is most willing to die for her belief. The Chorus comment that Antigone is like her father, a comparison which is made several times during the play, and that she has not learnt to yield in the face of misfortune. Creon pursues the same theme, but his remarks are heavy with unwitting irony since they are equally applicable to him:

Know that the most stubborn wills fall the furthest,
and that it is the strongest iron, tempered in the fire to hardness,
which you will see breaking and shattering the most.

                                                        (473-6)

He speaks of Antigone's *hubris* (insolent pride) and seems obsessed by the fact that she, a woman, has dared to defy him, a man.

Creon challenges Antigone as to how Eteocles would feel about Polyneices' burial, asserting that an *ekhthros* (enemy) does not become a *philos* (friend) when he dies. Antigone replies with the often quoted statement: ' It is not my nature to share in hatred, but to share in love' (523).

Creon's response is bitter and sexist:

> Go now down below the earth and love these men, if you must love.
> No woman will rule me as long as I live.
>
> (524-5)

Ismene, whom Creon assumes is also guilty, now wishes to share in Antigone's punishment but her sister will not allow it. Critics have regarded this scene as a violent rejection of Ismene by Antigone and have pointed out the irony in view of Antigone's assertion about her loving nature in line 523. However, a production at the National Theatre in London in 1983 showed the sisters embracing lovingly at this point and a close examination of the Greek text reveals only one line in which Antigone can be said to be definitely hostile. To Ismene's question: 'What pleasure is there in life for me deprived of you?' (548) Antigone replies: 'Ask Creon, for he is the one you care for' (549). But when Ismene protests at this, her sister instantly expresses regret: 'Indeed, I am giving myself pain in mocking you, if I am mocking' (550). The Greek scholar Jebb perceptively glossed this line: '...the taunt sprang from anguish, not from a wish to pain'.

Antigone sings a *kommos* with the Chorus as she begins her journey to the cave and her death. She interprets the Chorus' remarks as mockery and is filled with self-pity. This prompts the Elders to remark that Antigone overreached herself in boldness and they wonder whether her fate is linked to her father's. Mention of her father drives Antigone deeper into despair and the Chorus then declare:

> Authority is not to be overreached
> in the sight of the man who exercises authority.
> Your self-willed temper has destroyed you.
>
> (873-5)

At this Antigone returns to her opening theme: she is unwept and unwed; no loved one will mourn her. What of Haemon and Ismene, one may well ask? Antigone's self-absorption at this moment is complete.

(b) Creon

The audience's first encounter with Creon is when he announces his edict, prohibiting the burial of Polyneices' body. He states, with the irony so often employed by Sophocles:

> It is impossible to know fully the nature,
> the strength of will and judgement of any man
> until he has been shown engaged in ruling and making laws.
>
> (175-7)

He condemns anyone who places a *philos* (friend, relative) before his city and calls on all-seeing Zeus as his witness that he will always put the city first. Creon, unlike Antigone, will not give priority to his family or friends. He believes that his edict is made with the approval of the gods, and he reminds the citizens that Polyneices returned from exile wishing to destroy by fire his fatherland and the native gods. Therefore it is right that he should be denied burial. Creon claims that anyone who is *eunous* (well-intentioned) towards the city will agree with him, but points out that there are always some who are willing to do anything for money.

Creon is interrupted by the arrival of the Guard. His function and character have been much discussed and widely differing conclusions have been reached. Some commentators have regarded him as 'comic relief', designed to break the mounting tension of the play; others reject the notion that there was any place for comic figures in tragedy. Nonetheless, the Guard certainly acts as a foil to Creon and reveals more to the audience of the new ruler's 'nature, strength of will and judgement'. When Creon asks what the news is, the Guard replies:

> I want to speak to you first on my own behalf.
> For I neither did the deed nor saw whoever was the doer,
> nor should I justly fall into misfortune because of it.
>
> (238-40)

What does this tell us about Creon? That he was likely to react to bad news by blaming the bearer? Or is the Guard just generally fearful? Or is this exchange quite appropriate for a guard who knows that he has failed in his duty and a ruler who justifiably feels that he has been betrayed? Certainly, Creon's reaction when he does discover the news seems to confirm the Guard's fears:

> Understand this well, I swear to you
> that if you do not find and produce before my very eyes
> the man who carried out this burial,
> death alone will not be enough for you,
> until alive and hanging you will have revealed this plot,
> so that... you may learn
> that one should not be in love with profit
> from any and every source.
>
> (305-12)

Creon has jumped to conclusions. He is convinced that the guards have been bribed and that there are conspirators plotting against him (289-92). An interesting reaction, when one recalls Antigone's earlier insistence that the edict had been aimed personally at her.

The Chorus have other ideas, inspired by the Guard's claim that there were no traces of a spade or signs of wheel ruts and that the body had been untouched by dogs or birds: they suggest that the gods had a hand in the deed. Creon calls the Chorus *anous* (senseless), a word which Ismene earlier used of Antigone, and reiterates his view that the gods had no concern for Polyneices who had come to burn their temples. It has often been written that Creon puts his own man-made laws above the gods' laws and in fact this is the charge which Antigone makes in her confrontation with him. However, this is not what Creon actually believes or says. Rather he cannot accept that the gods of the city and the gods whom he worships would feel that a traitor such as Polyneices deserves a burial.

When Ismene reminds Creon of the fact that Antigone was to be the bride of Haemon, Creon's son, his immediate riposte is: 'There are other fields for him to plough' (569). Haemon himself appears not as a distraught lover pleading for his bride but as a self-controlled advocate of the sensible course. He says:

> Father I am yours...no marriage will be reckoned
> more important for me to have
> than your good guidance.
>
> (635-8)

Sophocles did not choose to include a scene between Haemon and Antigone and neither character refers to their love for the other. Yet it is by no means certain that Sophocles' version, in which Haemon commits suicide clasping the body of Antigone, was well-known to the original audience. There were several other versions of the Antigone story, including one treated by Euripides in which Creon ordered Haemon to kill Antigone but instead the son hid her in the countryside and later fathered her child. Some critics believe the Haemon–Antigone motif to be an important structural element of the play. They suggest that the subsequent choral ode on the power of Eros was intended to remind the audience of how Creon has set himself against a great cosmic force, sexual passion.

The debate between Haemon and Creon includes many of the themes of earlier scenes and focuses on Creon's style of ruling, clearly revealing his 'nature, strength of will and judgement'. Creon claims:

> Whoever the city has put in charge must be obeyed
> in the smallest matters, whether right or wrong.
>
> (666-7)

Three arguments are dominant in his speech – the city must be placed before one's family, a ruler must be obeyed, and men must not allow women to get the better of them. In reply Haemon assumes the role of spokesman for the citizens of Thebes:

> ...the city laments for this girl,
> because most undeserving of all women
> she is to die in the most cruel way
> for committing the most glorious deeds.
>
> (693-5)

He pleads with his father not to insist on having his own way but to be prepared to listen to others, and he uses images similar to those which Creon himself had employed to describe Antigone:

> You know how those trees which yield
> to the flooding waters of winter torrents
> preserve their smallest branches,
> but those which resist are destroyed,
> torn out by their roots.
> Similarly, a man who sails a ship,
> keeping the sheets tight and not yielding an inch,
> will soon be overturned
> and will finish the rest of his voyage
> with the rowing benches upside down.
>
> (712-17)

Creon is outraged that Haemon should lecture him and exclaims that the people of Thebes will not tell him how to rule. Haemon replies 'You would rule a deserted land beautifully, alone' (739) and accuses his father of '...trampling on the honours of the gods' (745). The view of Creon as a tyrannical extremist has been reinforced.

The scene with the blind prophet, Teiresias, serves as the final illumination of Creon's character and of the main themes of the play. It has been regarded by some as a pendant twinned with the Haemon/Creon scene, placed either side of Antigone's departure for the cave. Teiresias, it is true, like Haemon, warns Creon to change his mind; but the ruler's reaction has far more in common with his treatment of the Guard than that of his son. Creon accuses the prophet of having been bribed and he utters words which the audience must surely have regarded as blasphemy:

> Not even if the eagles of Zeus snatch at his body
> and wish to carry his flesh to the throne of Zeus,
> not even in fear of such pollution
> will I allow his burial.

(1040-3)

This statement is tempered in the very next line:

> For I know well that no mortal has the power
> to defile the gods.

(1043-4)

but its shocking impact would have already been made. Creon continues to insist that Teiresias has accepted a bribe. The prophet is finally driven to reveal that within the day the king will have paid for his deeds with the death of his child. After Teiresias has departed the Chorus persuade Creon to change his course.

This conversion has been criticised by some as being too sudden, but in any case it is to no avail. He carries out Teiresias' instructions in the wrong order and Antigone has committed suicide before he reaches her. The bitter rejection by Haemon and his suicide are swiftly followed by the suicide of Creon's wife, Eurydice. The King is alone and broken; he had learned wisdom too late. Creon has been punished, but he has also been found empty; he did not once remain true to his word within the play. The original penalty which he decreed was death by stoning; this he reduced to starvation in a cave outside of the city in order to avoid pollution. He threatened to kill Ismene, but did not; he gave way and buried Polyneices in the end. He forfeited his pride and his principles as well as his family and his status in the city. Antigone did not compromise at all, unless one views her final lament as a sign of weakness. She was determined to bury her brother and to die alone, and she does both. Nevertheless, although the gods punish Creon they do not save Antigone and the drama is focused more clearly on these two humans and their emotions than on divine will. Did Sophocles intend Creon to be seen as a ruthless, blaspheming tyrant or an insecure and inexperienced ruler trying vainly to prove his resolution? Should Antigone be regarded as a self-destructive martyr or as a loving heroine?

(c) Oedipus

There has been much debate about the character of Oedipus in *Oedipus Tyrannus* and whether his pride and his violent temper were tragic flaws in his personality which hastened his final downfall. Certainly, at the beginning of the play Oedipus is portrayed as the caring father and saviour of his people. The Priest appeals to him to rescue his city from the plague just as he had preserved it from the Sphinx. Oedipus tells his people:

> I do have pity for you, my children,
> and I know and am not ignorant of
> the things which you have come here desiring.
> For I know well that you are all suffering,
> and although you suffer, there is not one of you
> who suffers as much as I do.
> For a single grief comes to each one of you alone
> and nothing else. But my spirit
> is grieving for the city, for myself
> and for you all at the same time.
>
> (*Oedipus Tyrannus* 58-64)

The fact that he has already sent Creon to Apollo's oracle at Delphi for help is another indication of his concern.

Oedipus takes seriously the message which Creon brings and determines that he will find the murderer of Laius, the polluter of his city; he heaps dreadful curses on the head of the murderer or any who offer him shelter. In his quest for relief from the plague Oedipus had also sent for the old blind prophet Teiresias. In the encounter with him a new aspect of Oedipus is revealed, his violent temper. The King becomes exceptionally angry because the prophet refuses to reveal what he knows. He accuses the prophet of being involved in Laius' murder and taunts him with his blindness. When Teiresias retaliates with the truth Oedipus accuses him of accepting bribes and he boasts of his own skill:

> When the Sphinx, the doglike riddler-singer, was here,
> how was it that you did not say anything
> to bring release for the townspeople?
> ...But I came, Oedipus who knew nothing,
> I put a stop to her,
> finding the answer by intelligence...

(391-8)

Pride as well as anger is clearly displayed in this speech.

Oedipus also jumps to the conclusion that Creon is conspiring with Teiresias to overthrow him. He reacts equally violently towards him; he will not listen to his arguments or wait to find out the truth, asserting: 'I want to kill you, not to banish you' (623). Oedipus does not know the truth but he believes that he has intelligence and understanding. Creon stands in contrast to him, as is clearly shown when he says: 'I don't know; I usually keep silent on matters which I do not understand' (569). Jocasta's reference to the death of her husband, the old king Laius, at a crossroad prompts Oedipus to recall how he had killed several men at such a spot. He had lost his temper and violently murdered four or five people because someone had tried to jostle him out of the road; what is more, he does not seem to have given the affair a moment's thought since then. His *time* (honour) and esteem had been affronted; he had remedied the situation and saw no need to feel guilty. At the same time the audience is made aware of his unease about his parentage and his earlier eagerness to uncover the truth.

The Corinthian Messenger's explanation about how he had received the baby Oedipus makes Jocasta realise the dreadful truth and she goes to her death. Oedipus is now excited and elated at the prospect of discovering his origins and he reacts unkindly to her departure. He assumes that she is worried by the possibility that he may be a slave's child and exclaims:

> She thinks that she is a great lady
> and is ashamed at my low birth.

(1078-9)

The penultimate victim of Oedipus' violent temper is the old Servant who is unwilling to confirm that the man before him is the son of Laius and Jocasta. Oedipus threatens him with torture if he will not speak. The scene is similar to that with Teiresias: a refusal to supply information ignites Oedipus' rage and the result is a revelation which he may have preferred not to hear. The final victim of Oedipus' anger is himself – he stabs his eyes in desperate fury, appalled at the crimes he has committed against his family. He explains that he was determined to inflict a terrible punishment on himself and to prevent himself, even after death, from having to see the father and mother whom he had so defiled.

But the picture of Oedipus which Sophocles chose to present in the final scene echoes that of the first – Oedipus the caring father, worried about the future for his children and longing to embrace his daughters. Oedipus' behaviour was not always admirable but his fate was preordained.He had already unwittingly committed patricide and incest, fulfilling the oracle. He has faults of character, a hot temper and pride, but an audience cannot help but sympathise with him in his plight.

The role of the chorus

Some critics have suggested that in Sophocles' tragedies the chorus becomes another actor, rather than maintaining its traditional roles. Other scholars dispute this, but none doubt that Sophocles integrated his chorus more fully into his plays than Aeschylus did. The chorus of the *Antigone* consist of Theban elders; their odes are definitely in a different register and deal mainly with background issues and mythological parallels. Their reaction to Creon's proclamation is muted; they acknowledge his power to enforce whatever laws he pleases and have no desire to risk their lives by disobedience. After the Guard has described Polyneices' mysterious burial the Chorus leader voices a thought which may have occurred to the audience or which Sophocles may have wished to suggest to the audience – was it the work of the gods? The closing lines of their subsequent ode praise the man who is obedient to the laws and declare that whoever boldly commits evil will be *apolis* (without a city). This seems to refer to the person who has buried the body and to echo Creon's earlier sentiments about putting the city before the individual and obeying the laws, but it could equally well apply to Creon himself who has dared beyond what is permitted and has lost the support of the citizens.

The Chorus show little sympathy for Antigone after her capture, commenting that she is wild and obstinate like her father. Their later reference to the curse of the house of Labdacus implies that the girl is doomed. During the debate between Creon and Haemon they agree with both, but once Haemon has rushed off it is left to the Chorus leader to underline the possibilty that the young man may do himself violence. At this point too, the information that only Antigone is to be punished is

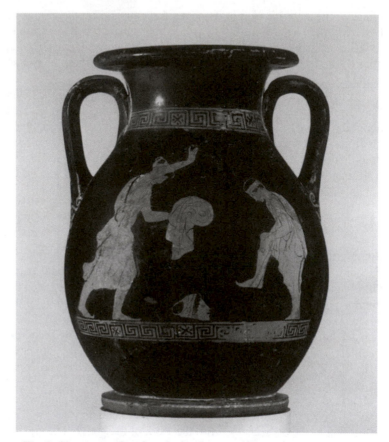

Fig. 8 Chorus men dressing, depicted on a red-figure vase.

elicited from Creon by the Chorus. The ensuing ode on the theme of unconquerable, irresistible Love blames Eros for the strife between father and son. It is immediately followed by the *kommos* scene; the Chorus' attitude towards Antigone at this point has been interpreted in different ways. Some commentators suggest that the presence of Creon frightens the Chorus into not expressing their true feelings; others point out the dramatic necessity for Antigone to be isolated and alone at this juncture. The choice of male, elderly citizens as the Chorus has automatically distanced them from the young, passionate female and seems to place them on the side of Creon's law and order. The Chorus' only positive intervention in the play occurs when they urge Creon to accept Teiresias' advice.

The Chorus of the *Oedipus Tyrannus* take a more positive role. They elicit more sympathy for Oedipus by declaring that they will remain loyal to him; he had saved them from the Sphinx and they will not condemn him now without clear proof. During the quarrel between Oedipus and Creon the Chorus urge the King to accept Creon's word and they try to stop the argument. This is apparently a firm intervention on Creon's behalf but at the same time they reiterate their devotion to Oedipus:

> Know that I would be out of my right mind...
> If I turned away from you who set on the right path
> my beloved land when it was struggling among troubles...
>
> *(Oedipus Tyrannus* 690-5)

Jocasta's rejection of oracles shocks the Chorus; they call on Zeus to witness that Apollo's oracles are no longer respected and they assert that 'the honour due to the gods is gone' (910). Once the truth is known the Chorus show sympathy for Oedipus but they wish that they had never seen him. Their final words in the play were not original but they were appropriate: 'call no man happy until he is dead.'

The choral odes of the *Oedipus Tyrannus* offer a much closer commentary on the action of the play than those of the *Antigone*, but the odes of both plays are all concerned with the gods in some way. Sophocles' choruses retained the role of mediator between gods and men and between the characters in the drama and the audience.

The gods and fate

No gods appear on stage in the *Antigone* and the *Oedipus Tyrannus* but their views are interpreted by the human characters and they are often appealed to by the chorus. As was noted earlier, in the *Antigone* both main characters at first believe that they are abiding by the gods' wishes. But as Antigone goes to her death she feels despair and some doubt:

> What law of the gods have I broken?
> ...But if these things are good in the sight of the gods,
> I may gain pardon for my sins as I suffer.
>
> *(Antigone* 921-6)

Throughout the play the Chorus make reference to the need to honour the gods and to the inevitability of destiny. This proves to be true and although Creon blames himself entirely he recognises that it was a god who actually punished him (1273). The Chorus reinforce this in the closing lines of the play with the warning: 'One must not commit sacrilege against the gods' (1349).

The question of whether Fate or personal responsibility dominates the course of events in the *Oedipus Tyrannus* is a matter for debate. However, it cannot be disputed that the presence of Apollo is felt throughout the play. In the opening scene we learn of the plague which is afflicting Thebes, and although Apollo is not mentioned by name at this stage he was the god often associated with mysterious plagues. Oedipus then tells his people that he has sent Creon to the oracle of Apollo for advice. After Creon has reported Apollo's words Oedipus appears to be full of respect for the god. He tells Creon that he will search for Laius' murderer assiduously: '...taking vengeance on behalf of this country and on behalf of Apollo at the same time' (*Oedipus Tyrannus* 136) and he seems to view himself as the god's agent. The choral ode immediately after this scene is a prayer to Apollo the Deliverer.

When Oedipus falsely accuses Teiresias, he retorts:

> Fate will not fall upon you from my hands,
> since Apollo himself has the power
> and it is his concern to achieve these things.
>
> (376-7)

Later Jocasta attempts to calm Oedipus by discrediting oracles and prophets:

> Listen to me and learn...
> that no mortal has any skill of prophecy
> ...An oracle once came to Laius,
> I will not say from Phoebus himself,
> but from his assistants...
>
> (708-12)

She does not, however, commit blasphemy at this point, rather she adds:

> The god himself would easily make clear
> those things for which he has identified a need.
>
> (724-5)

Jocasta's story prompts Oedipus to recall how he had murdered a man at a place where three roads met. The reason for his journey was Apollo: he had gone to Delphi to ask Apollo about his parents and had set out on the road to Thebes after learning from the god that he was destined to murder his father and marry his mother. Once more Jocasta casts doubt

on oracles, this time including Apollo in her scepticism. The Chorus sing
in horror at the lack of respect for the gods.

The news from Corinth leads Oedipus to join Jocasta in doubting
the veracity of prophets and oracles:

> Alas wife, what consideration should one give
> to the hearth of the Pythian prophet
> or to the birds screaming above?...
> Polybus has taken the oracles with him,
> lying in Hades, worth nothing.

(964-72)

Soon Jocasta realises that the oracles were true; Oedipus takes longer to
comprehend but when he does he punishes himself by stabbing his eyes.
This self-blinding was not foretold by either of the oracles, but it was
predicted by Teiresias, Apollo's servant, as he described himself. When
questioned by the Chorus about it Oedipus replies:

> It was Apollo, Apollo, my friends,
> who brought about these evil, evil sufferings of mine.
> But no other man's hand struck me,
> I in my wretchedness struck myself.

(1329-31)

Oedipus seems to be accepting Apollo's control of his fate but
claiming some personal responsibity as well. Was the *Oedipus Tyrannus* intended to remind the audience of man's essential ignorance
and that knowledge can only belong to the gods? Commentators have
pointed out Apollo's connection with self-knowledge: 'know yourself' was inscribed on his temple at Delphi. The themes of plague
and the disruption of natural order can also be linked to Apollo. He
was the symbol of harmonious nature as well as the healer, and
Oedipus is set against Apollo, nature and civilised society by the
enormity of his unnatural acts. Finally, one is left with the question
'Can oracles ever be evaded?' The outcome of the *Oedipus Tyrannus*
suggests that Sophocles did not think so.

Language, imagery and irony

There are several themes which are repeated and developed in the
language of the *Antigone*: for example, the *philos, ekhthros* (friend,
enemy) and *eunous, anous* (of sound mind or well-intentioned, senseless) vocabulary which was mentioned above. The idea of correct

control, using the word *orthos* and its compounds, also occurs some seventeen times. The symbol of the ship of state and associated nautical imagery, most appropriate to the Athenians whose power was sea-based, appears several times (e.g. 189-90, 715-7, 994), although caution must again be advised for the Greekless reader since the image occurs far less often in the original text than in some modern translations. Irony is also to be found, especially in the speeches of Creon, and some examples were commented on earlier in the discussion of his character. In this section, however, I shall concentrate on the *Oedipus Tyrannus*.

There are countless instances of word play and irony within the text of the *Oedipus Tyrannus* and they cannot all be examined individually here. Word play on the name Oedipus pervades the tragedy. The Greek name *Oidipous* was given to the baby because the pinning of his ankles had caused his feet to swell (1036) – the Greek verb *oidein* means to be swollen and the word for foot is *pous*. However, Sophocles also exploits other aspects of the name. *Dipous* means two-footed and echoes the Sphinx's riddle (what goes on four feet in the morning, two at noon and three in the evening?). Foot imagery occurs throughout the play (e.g. 130, 418, 468, 479, 718, 866 & 878). But a much stronger association is made with the first two syllables, connecting them with the Greek verb *oida*, I know, and all the irony implicit in that, since Oedipus does not know who he is and what he has done. *Oida* and its compounds are used at least 74 times in the course of the drama and about half of these words are spoken by Oedipus himself. Often the expression is heavy with double, or occasionally, triple, meaning. For example, Oedipus boasts to Teiresias of his superior intelligence in having solved the riddle of the Sphinx; he declares, sarcastically as he thinks: 'I, Oedipus, who knew nothing put a stop to her' (*Oedipus Tyrannus* 397).

Connected with this theme of knowledge and ignorance is that of blindness and sight. Teiresias is blind but he sees the truth. At first he is unwilling to reveal what he knows and this drives Oedipus to accuse the prophet of involvement in the crime:

> Know that it seems to me
> that you had a hand in contriving this
> ...if you happened to have sight
> I would even say that the deed was yours alone.

> (346-9)

Teiresias retaliates, declaring:

I say that you do not know that you are living shamefully
with those most closely related to you,
and that you do not see what an evil state you are in.

(366-7)

Oedipus cruelly counter-attacks:

You are blind in your ears, your mind and your eyes.

(371)

Teiresias replies with unerring accuracy that men will soon be hurling
such taunts at Oedipus and he later states this even more explicitly:

...you have mocked me for my blindness.
You have sight but you do not see
the evil state you are in...
A terrible-footed curse will drive you out of this land,
you who now see clearly will then see darkness.

(412-19)

This is repeated once more before the prophet leaves, clearly underlining
the importance of the theme (454-6), and the imagery is sustained right
to the end of the play.

Irony is one of Sophocles' main tools in his treatment of the story,
irony both in the broad outlines of the development of the plot and in the
phrases and even individual words spoken by the characters. Throughout
the play characters do or say things, thinking that they are helping
someone or performing a good deed and the reverse turns out to be true.
This could be applied to Oedipus' actions fifteen years before: seeking
to spare his father, his mother and himself and to avoid his destiny, he
walked right into it. Similarly, at the beginning of the play, in an effort
to alleviate his people's sufferings from the plague, he sends Creon to
Apollo's oracle for advice and summons Teiresias. Both of these actions
lead to his eventual self-knowledge and downfall. In the third scene
Jocasta, in an effort to set his mind at rest and to prove that there is no
truth in prophecy, tells Oedipus how Laius was killed at the place where
three roads meet. However, the description of the location prompts
Oedipus to suspect that he may, after all, have killed Laius. The
Messenger who comes from Corinth in the fourth scene hopes to remove
Oedipus' fear of marrying his mother by telling him that Merope was
not his mother and that he had been cast out from Laius' house as a baby.
But this leads to Jocasta's immediate recognition of the truth and her
suicide and eventually causes Oedipus to discover who he is.

Some of the lines uttered in the play must have left the audience gasping at their dreadful accuracy, while the speakers remained oblivious of their import. An example of such dramatic irony occurs in the first scene when the Priest says of Oedipus:

> ...we judge you to be the first of men
> both in the disasters of life and in the dealings of the gods.
>
> (33-4)

and when Oedipus states in reply:

> ...there is not one of you
> who suffers equally with me.
>
> (60-1)

But these unwitting *double-entendres* are subtle indeed compared to Oedipus' remarks concerning Laius, knowing neither that he had killed him nor that he was his father. He declares:

> I shall speak as a stranger to this story
> and as a stranger to the deed...
>
> (219)

and later adds:

> ...I will fight on his behalf
> as if he were my own father...
>
> (264-5)

When Oedipus asks Jocasta what Laius was like, she replies in innocence: 'He was not very different from you in appearance' (743). Oedipus' thoughts about his parentage: 'I consider myself to be a child of Fortune *(Tyche)*...' (1080), turn out to be a most appropriate description.

In the *Oedipus Tyrannus* Oedipus makes the journey from mental blindness to self-knowledge, at the same time changing from a man who is supremely confident of his intelligence to a physically self-blinded wretch. He believed that he was a Corinthian stranger, but he finds out that he is a true-born Theban; he believed that he was the man who could save the city, but he turns out to be the cause of its pollution and instead of being King of Thebes he becomes an outcast.

Conclusion

Sophocles seems to have been concerned with how humans reacted to crises and dilemmas. The gods have their part to play but the mortal characters make decisions of their own. The poet does not present any simple answers to the problems facing his characters; neither Antigone nor Creon are wholly in the right. Antigone is wilfully defiant and self-destructive, while Creon sincerely believes that he is acting correctly by putting the interests of the state above those of his family or of a traitor. Oedipus is equally misguided in his search for the truth, although in his case the truth may have been inescapable.

Sophocles was also a skilful poet. His subtle use of words and images reinforces the underlying themes of his plays. His capacity for composition was undiminished by age and it is recorded that he defended himself in court at the age of ninety, when his sons were attempting to gain control of the family property on the grounds of his senility, by reciting an ode from the *Oedipus at Colonus* which he was just writing. The jury applauded and declared him unquestionably sane.

Chapter 5
Euripides

The poet and his works

Euripides, the youngest of the three great fifth-century tragedians, has always been the most controversial. Born in either 485/4 or 480 BC (sources differ) he grew up in Athens at a time of tremendous change and expansion. The league of allied cities, ever increasing in number, was becoming more like an Athenian empire; the final moves towards full democracy (in theory at least) were being made; artists and thinkers from all over the Greek world were coming to settle in Athens. Euripides is thought to have associated with two philosophers in particular, Anaxagoras and Protagoras. The claims made in comic fragments and in the *Life* that Socrates helped Euripides to write his plays are undoubtedly false but they do reflect a view that the poet was influenced by philosophers. As Athens became embroiled in the long war with Sparta (431-404 BC the zeal for new ideas was replaced by disillusion and Euripides must have been affected by this.

Euripides entered his first competition in 455 BC and he is known to have taken part in 22 Dionysiac festivals. He must, therefore, have written at least 88 plays; 18 of these have survived more or less complete: *Alcestis* (produced instead of a satyr play in 438 BC), *Medea* (431 BC), *Heraclidae* (*Children of Heracles* c. 430 BC), *Hippolytus* (428 BC), *Andromache* (c. 425 BC), *Hecabe* (c. 424 BC), *Supplices* (*Suppliant Women* c. 423 BC), *Ion* (c. 418 BC), *Electra* (c. 417-413 BC), *Heracles* (c. 417 BC), *Troades* (*Trojan Women* c. 415 BC), *Iphigenia in Tauris* (c. 413 BC), *Helen* (c. 412 BC), *Cyclops* (satyr play c. 412 BC), *Phoenissae* (*Phoenician Women* c. 411-409 BC), *Orestes* (408 BC), *Iphigenia in Aulis* (produced posthumously 405 BC), *Bacchae* (produced posthumously, 405 BC). However, he won only four victories and one of these was posthumous.

This apparent unpopularity has provided a fertile field for discussion. Is the fact that he was chosen to present an entry at the festival of Dionysus 22 times evidence of his popularity or does the fact that he was not chosen every single year after 455 BC indicate

Fig. 9 Euripides.

unpopularity? He is known to have spent the last two years of his life (408-406 BC) in 'exile' at the court of King Archelaus at Pella. Was he encouraged to leave Athens or did he leave on his own initiative prompted by the desperate state of Athenian affairs at that time? Ancient biographers claim that he was a recluse who composed his plays in a cave on the sea shore. But elsewhere in the ancient sources we are told that one of Protagoras' works had its first reading at Euripides' house and in Aristophanes' *Acharnians* (425 BC we see the hero Dikaiopolis visiting Euripides at his house where he is busy composing a tragedy.

Euripides and Aristophanes

Indeed Euripides' appearances as a character in Aristophanes' comedies have been cited by some critics as proof of his unpopularity in the fifth century. However, others have detected a genuine affection and appreciation in the comic poet's portrayals of Euripides. Whatever the reason, Euripides is certainly depicted in three of Aristophanes' eleven extant comedies and in each the humour of the situation depends upon the audience being very familiar with the works of the tragic poet.

The *Acharnians* is the first play in which we see him and here he is the hero's natural choice for inspiration, costume and props when he decides to offer his head to the chorus if he cannot persuade them that war with the Spartans is a bad idea. This is a parody of Euripides' *Telephos* (now lost) in which King Telephos vowed that he would speak his mind even if he was killed for it. Apparently, Euripides had presented Telephos dressed in rags (another reference is made to this in the later *Frogs*), but, according to Aristophanes in the *Acharnians*, he had also dressed Oeneus, Phoenix, Philoctetes, Bellerophon, Thyestes and Ino in similar fashion! There are additional jokes about Euripides' use of the *mechane* (crane), his depiction of cripples in his plays and his connection with greengrocery. Professor Gilbert Murray (a Classical scholar of the early part of this century) gave a very plausible explanation of how the stock jibe about Euripides' mother being a greengrocer may have developed in his book, *Euripides and His Age*.

Euripides is a central figure in Aristophanes' *Thesmophoriazusae* (*The Poet and the Women*, 411 BC); in fact he is the *raison d'etre* for the play. The women, meeting in an assembly at the women's festival, the Thesmophoria, are planning to punish Euripides dreadfully for the way in which he has depicted them in his tragedies and, according to Aristophanes, for betraying all their secrets to men. Euripides persuades an elderly relative, Mnesilochus, to dress up as a woman, infiltrate the assembly and defend him. Unfortunately, his disguise is uncovered. Using ploys from Euripides' *Telephos* and *Palamedes* he summons the poet himself to help. The second part of the comedy consists of a series of rescue attempts by Euripides, using ideas from his plays and involving lengthy parodies of their verses. He pretends to be Menelaus rescuing Helen and Perseus, riding in on the crane, trying to save Andromeda. Just as in the *Acharnians* Euripides' inspiration and equipment saved Dikaiopolis' skin, so in the *Thesmophoriazusae* the poet is able to persuade the women to give him another chance. However, Euripides' portrayal of women and use of the crane are not the only features of his plays which are commented on in the *Thesmophoriazusae*. One woman tells how her husband had died on the military expedition to Cyprus and how she has five children to bring up; her trade is selling myrtle wreathes (used at sacrifices to the gods) in the market but now:

> This man in his tragedies makes men deny
> that there are any gods,
> so that I no longer earn even half as much!
>
> (449-51)

Euripides' supposed lack of belief in the traditional gods is also depicted in Aristophanes' *Frogs* (405 BC). Once more the tragic poet is central to the theme. The god Dionysus explains at the beginning of the comedy how he is desperate to fetch a good tragic poet back from Hades and that he has a longing for Euripides. He gives two reasons for his choice of Euripides, first because:

> Euripides, being a versatile rogue,
> would have a go at making it back here with me.
>
> (80-1)

and secondly, he is looking for:

> ...a truly creative poet who can utter a noble phrase
>
> (96-7)

It is true that Heracles suggests that Sophocles is a better poet and that Aeschylus wins the contest in the end, but this does not mean that Euripides is denigrated throughout. His atheism is parodied when he tells Dionysus that he prays to 'other gods' and he declaims:

> Ether, my nourishment, and Pivot of my Tongue,
> and Intelligence and keen-scented Nostrils,
> prove me correct in all the arguments I employ.
>
> (892-5)

As was stated in Chapter 3 the poets' criticisms of each other in the *Frogs* are clearly exaggerated for comic effect, but they must also have had some basis in fact or the audience would not have found them amusing. Euripides is made to boast of the clarity of his language and his use of the prologue to explain everything to the audience. He says that he made sure that everyone spoke in his plays, women, both old and young, slaves and masters (949-50). From his example the Athenian citizens had learned how to apply logic to their own daily affairs. Aeschylus responds by criticising Euripides for portraying immoral women and for introducing unheroic characters whose speech was as ragged as their costumes.

Nonetheless, one must treat such parodies and criticisms in ancient comedy with some caution. In both the *Thesmophoriazusae* and the *Frogs* there is a scathing reference to the famous line from the *Hippolytus* where Hippolytus tells the Nurse that his tongue swore and not his heart (612) and yet as the whole play has survived we know that Hippolytus actually stuck to his oath resolutely and did not reveal the truth about Phaedra even when Theseus threatened dire punishment. Lines and ideas taken out of context can be misleading. Our impression of Socrates would be quite different if Aristophanes' *Clouds* had survived but not the works of Plato and Xenophon. What we can deduce from Aristophanes' comedies is that Euripides' tragedies were familiar enough to the audience for them to recognise parodies of them and find them funny.

Those ideas and effects of Euripides which excited comment and criticism from Aristophanes and other ancient writers have remained equally controversial in modern times. He has been described as both a woman-hater and as an early feminist; he has been called an atheist and one with deeply held religious convictions; he has been seen as a realist determined to relate the tragic action of traditional myths to life in fifth-century Athens and as one whose characters are so unheroic as to be banal or absurd; he is credited with penetrating psychological insight in his portrayal of human emotions and accused of sacrificing character to rhetoric. Some critics read his plays as anti-war propaganda, others find in them stirring defences of Athens and her policies. Add to this the fact that Euripides' prologues have been criticised for telling the whole story before the play has started, that his endings have been censured because they are 'happy' or because a god implausibly appears and announces a solution and that, following Aristotle (*Poetics*, 1456a25-7), it has been suggested that Euripides did not integrate his choruses fully into the drama, and one has a fair summary of Euripidean scholarship.

I shall pursue some of these themes through a more detailed examination of the plays, in particular, the *Medea*, *Hippolytus* and the *Bacchae* (*Electra* will be dealt with in Chapter 6).

Prologues

The elderly Nurse is used to deliver the prologue of the *Medea*. She not only sets the scene but also reminds the audience of Medea's capacity for evil and prepares them for the shocking outcome of the play. She regrets that Medea should ever have met Jason and refers to her responsibilty for the death of Pelias and to her current status as an exile in Corinth. The Nurse explains that although Medea has been a loving and obedient wife Jason has now abandoned her and their sons and has married the daughter of Creon, the king of Corinth. She describes Medea's reaction and comments:

> She hates her sons and takes no pleasure in seeing them.
> I am afraid that she may be considering some new plan...
>
> (*Medea* 36-7)

Almost immediately the boys themselves appear with their Tutor, as if to underline the importance that they are to have in the play. The Nurse in fact repeats her fears for the children's safety three times before the Chorus appear and Medea herself is heard cursing the children offstage. In this way Euripides establishes at the outset what are to be the main themes of his play: Medea's passion and the violence of her temper; her status as a woman and a foreigner; Jason's expedient attitude to his marriage; the importance of children (shown in Aigeus' concern for his childlessness as well as by Medea's choice of punishment for Jason). The more traditional version of the Medea myth seems to have been that the Corinthians murdered the children. Whether Euripides' version of the story was his own has been hotly debated by scholars, but the weight of opinion now seems to support the view that he did invent Medea's murder of the children. This was an especially radical departure in 431 BC when Athens and Corinth were embarking on a war. However, the opening scene would certainly have prepared the audience for the novel twist.

Three years later the prologue of the *Hippolytus* went even further. The goddess Aphrodite introduced this play, revealing her identity in an uncompromising fashion:

> Great among mortals and not inglorious among the gods,
> I am called the Cyprian goddess.
> Of men...I give preference
> to those who revere my power,
> and I bring to ruin those
> who show proud resistance towards me.
>
> (1-6)

She explains that she has been scheming for a long time to cause Hippolytus' downfall and that it will be achieved this very day. She has made the boy's stepmother, Phaedra, fall in love with him and she will die:

> But this love must not perish in secret;
> I shall reveal the matter to Theseus and it will be exposed.
> The father will kill the young man who is so hostile to me,
> with the curses which his father Poseidon, Lord of the sea,
> granted to him, Theseus, as a favour ...
> Phaedra's honour will be saved but she must die.
>
> (41-8)

Euripides has here revealed almost the entire plot of his play. A modern audience might wonder why they should stay to see it, but to the Greeks the elements of surprise and suspense were not of major importance; how the poet would present the story was of greater interest.

The *Bacchae* is Euripides' last play – here too the prologue is delivered by a god, this time by Dionysus. He introduces himself and explains why he has come to Thebes. He is introducing his worship to Greece and has driven the women of Thebes from their homes in a frenzy as punishment for refusing to believe that Zeus was the father of Semele's child Dionysus. Pentheus, who has taken over the throne from the aging Cadmus, excludes Dionysus from prayers. The god is determined to prove his divinity and then he will depart; however, if the Thebans take up arms against his Bacchants he will fight back. As in the *Medea* we are given a hint of trouble to come, although there is a possibility of a peaceful outcome. Dionysus has asserted his divine power as Aphrodite did in the *Hippolytus* but it is by no means certain what will happen. Indeed, throughout the play Dionysus offers Pentheus opportunities to relent and tries to persuade him against using force.

Women

Women have important roles in all three of these tragedies. Moreover, each play contains speeches which are a damning indictment of the female sex and which are commonly quoted to illustrate Euripides' prejudice against women.

(a) Medea

Medea dominates her play totally: she appears in every scene after the prologue and outwits each of the male characters in turn. She also delivers a series of five monologues revealing to the Chorus and the audience her innermost thoughts and explaining to them her point of view. The Nurse and the Chorus of Corinthian Women sympathise with Medea for the majority of the tragedy and this helps to direct the audience's sympathy towards her. In the prologue the Nurse comments on Medea's submissiveness to Jason:

> She gives way to Jason in everything.
> This is the best means of keeping safe in marriage,
> when the woman does not disagree with the man.

> (13-15)

Whether irony was intended here or not is impossible to tell, but the speech reflects a commonly held view of Athenian marriage if not of Medea. Certainly the picture which Medea herself paints of marriage is far from attractive:

> Of all things which have life and intelligence
> we women are the most wretched.
> First it is necessary for us to buy a husband
> for an excessive amount of money,
> then to take him as master of our body –
> an even more distressing evil.
> Then, and this is the greatest point for debate,
> have we taken a bad man or a good one?
> It is not respectable for women to initiate divorce,
> nor are we able to send away the man.
> Coming amongst new customs and laws,
> it is necessary to be a prophet to know
> how to treat one's bed-partner,
> since one has not been taught at home.
> If, as a result of our hard work,
> a husband lives happily with us
> and does not react violently to the marriage yoke,
> our life is to be envied.
> If not, death would be better.
> But as for the man, whenever he is weary
> of the company of those at home,
> he can go out and put a stop to his heart's longings.
> But for us it is necessary to look to one man only.
> They say that we live a life free from danger at home,
> while they fight with spears.
> They do not understand.

> I would rather stand three times with a shield in battle
> than once give birth to a child!
>
> (230-51)

This speech has been the subject of much controversy – why is it given to a woman who was not an Athenian or even a Greek and who had not gone through an arranged marriage with a dowry? Was it intended to win more sympathy from the Chorus who had originally said of Medea:

> If your husband is devoting himself to a new bride
> it is his business.
>
> (155-7)

– a statement which proves the veracity of Medea's remarks about the acceptability of men finding comfort elsewhere. But why should the women in Aristophanes' comedy have objected to Euripides if this was how he presented their case? How would the predominantly male Athenian audience have reacted to this speech – was there a tacit understanding that men fought for the city while women provided the next generation of soldiers? Was Euripides deliberately challenging the audience and criticising the way in which Athenian males dominated the lives of their wives and daughters? But Medea's views would only have received serious consideration from the audience if they regarded her as a sympathetic character; even some modern scholars have regarded Medea as nothing more than a manic and wicked woman.

The woman's traditional roles in marriage are alluded to elsewhere in the play. In Medea's first scene with Jason, where she gives full rein to her anger, she refers to the need for women to produce sons and admits that childlessness would have been a reason for setting her aside:

> ...wicked man, you have betrayed me;
> you sought a new marriage bed although I had borne sons.
> If you were still childless it would be pardonable
> for you to have desired this other marriage.
>
> (488-91)

In response to Medea's later taunt that a foreign wife was no longer respectable, Jason makes a revealing reply. He says that he did not marry into the royal family because of the woman involved but because of the financial security (593-7). Marriage was a business transaction not a love match.

In her scenes with Creon and Aigeus and at the second meeting with Jason, Medea becomes almost a caricature of a woman. She weeps, touches their knees as a sign of humble supplication and begs for favours. She utters remarks such as:

We women, I won't say we are evil,
but we are what we are...

(889-90)

and: 'The female sex is naturally prone to tears' (928). However, after each of these men has left she announces triumphantly that she has been merely feigning subservience in order to further her plot for vengeance. Euripides does allow a softer side of Medea to appear in the scenes where she is torn over her decision to murder her children and where she describes the sweetness of their bodies and the love she feels for them. But her desire to wound Jason as deeply as possible by depriving him of his sons overcomes her maternal instincts.

Three of the choral odes in the *Medea* are closely concerned with the status and reputation of women. After Medea has organised her refuge in Athens she declares, uncharacteristically and probably with intentional irony for those able to recognise it:

Besides we were born women,
completely useless for noble deeds
but most clever contrivers of all wickedness.

(407-9)

The Chorus respond with an ode on how things will soon be reversed, since men are now engaging in deceitful plans. They point out that women and men are equally capable of wickedness, but male poets have always glorified men and vilified women:

Honour is coming for the female race.
No longer will malicious rumour keep us in subjection.
The Muses of old-fashioned singers will cease
to celebrate my faithlessness.
For Phoebus Apollo, the Lord of songs,
did not grant inspiration for lyric odes to our <female> mind.

(419-26)

Odd words from a male poet and certainly not the sentiments of a woman-hater.

The Chorus' fifth formal ode begins, rather strangely, with a general reflection on women's intelligence:

> I have often gone through more subtle arguments
> and engaged in greater conflict
> than the female race should in pursuing enquiries.
> But we also have a Muse
> which communicates with us on questions of wisdom,
> although it does not come to all of us –
> indeed you would perhaps find only a few
> of this sort among many women.

> (1081-8)

Is there yet more irony here or is Euripides' comment to be taken at face value? It is commonly said that playwrights used the chorus for communicating their own thoughts to the audience, but how seriously would this Chorus of Corinthian Women have been taken by the audience?

There are, of course, unambiguously anti-women statements in the *Medea* but these are expressed by Jason whose attitude to women is extreme and who is not a very admirable character. During his first confrontation with Medea he declares that her hostility is based on sexual jealousy and adds:

> Humans should produce children in some other way
> and there should not be a female race;
> then there would be no evil for mankind.

> (573-5)

This cannot be regarded as a serious suggestion by Euripides, even though a similar sentiment occurs in the *Hippolytus*. Surely such a statement is intended to show the extent of Jason's anger and prejudice and how unable or unwilling he is to cope with a relationship with a woman (compare his statement about his new marriage (593-7) mentioned earlier)? In the final scene, as Medea out of reach in her chariot taunts him, Jason once more refers to sexual jealousy: 'Did you think it right to murder them because of a marriage bed?' (1367). Medea replies that such a thing is not insignificant to a woman; Jason retorts that it is to a self-restrained woman. He does not condemn the whole race, just Medea.

(b) Hippolytus

The version which we have of the *Hippolytus* is Euripides second treatment of the theme. His first had been universally reviled because the character of Phaedra was so scandalous. In our version it is established right from the prologue that Phaedra is the innocent victim of Aphrodite, merely the tool of the goddess. Phaedra is intent upon an honourable death and she cannot be regarded as an exemplar of the wickedness of the human race. any trouble she causes for Hippolytus is the work of Aphrodite. On the other hand, Hippolytus is not a particularly admirable character: he is exclusive in his worship of Artemis and he seems to be afraid of women and sex.

Phaedra explains that she knew that her love for Hippolytus was a sin and that as she could not conquer it she had determined to die. She adds:

> Besides, I knew well that I was a woman,
> an object of contempt to all.

(406-7)

She then curses the woman who was first unfaithful to her husband and brought disgrace on womankind. Phaedra is not saying that all women *are* shameless and contemptible. She is saying that women are *regarded as* contemptible (by men?) and that those who have committed adultery have brought trouble for other women.

It is Hippolytus' condemnation of women which is most often quoted from this play as evidence of Euripides' own attitude to women. The speech is made in a fit of horror after the Nurse has revealed Phaedra's love to him:

> O Zeus, why did you bring women, a deceitful evil for men,
> into the light of the sun?
> If you wanted to breed a human race,
> it was not necessary to produce it from women.
> Men could have dedicated as offerings in your temples
> either gold or iron or a weight of bronze
> to buy the seed of children, each of the appropriate value,
> and lived in homes free from women.
> But now as soon as we bring the evil pest into our homes
> we drain the wealth out of our house.
> From this it is clear what a great evil woman is –
> for the father who produces her and brings her up
> provides a dowry and sends her away from home
> so that he can be free of the pest.
> On the other hand, the one who receives
> the accursed creature into his house rejoices.

He give beautiful ornaments and honour to the most evil
creature
and, poor wretch, works hard to provide her with dresses,
draining away the wealth of his house.
He has no choice;
the man who is glad because he has made a marriage alliance
with a noble family of in-laws
makes the best of a bitter marriage bed,
whereas the one who has a good wife but poverty-stricken
in-laws
reckons that his bad fortune is outweighed by the good.
The easiest way is to marry some nobody;
but a woman set on a pedestal at home
because of her simple-mindedness is not a benefit.
I hate a clever woman.
May there never be a woman in my house
who thinks more than a woman should.
Aphrodite gives rise to wickedness more in clever women,
whereas the witless woman is less prone to foolishness
because of her lack of intelligence.
No servant should ever come near to a woman,
but wild beasts that are unable to speak
should live with them so that they are not able to talk to
anyone...
Curse you all! I will never have enough of hating women,
even if people say that I always say the same thing,
for they are always evil.
Either let someone teach them self-control
or let me always attack them.

(616-68)

This speech is clearly a very emotional outburst full of fanatical hostility
to women. The last line is ironic because the ability to exert self-control
(*sophronein*) is the very thing which Hippolytus himself lacks. His
obsession with chastity is excessive and his rejection of love and the
female sex is extreme. The audience's sympathies at this point must
surely lie with Phaedra, who has been betrayed by the Nurse as well as
being manipulated by Aphrodite, and Hippolytus' tirade cannot be
viewed as a serious anti-feminist message. However, reading it in
conjunction with Medea's speech about marriage one might conclude
that Euripides had a rather cynical view of marriage as an institution and

regarded it as bringing little joy to either party. Phaedra's immediate response to Hippolytus' outburst is to lament: 'How wretched and ill-starred are the fates of women!' (669-70). But this must be taken in context as a reaction to Hippolytus' remarks rather than being quoted in a vacuum as evidence that Euripides believed that women were an unfortunate race.

The female characters that are less than honourable in the Hippolytus are the goddesses, Aphrodite and Artemis; but I shall discuss their portrayal later as immortals rather than women.

(c) Bacchae

As Phaedra was the innocent tool of Aphrodite in the *Hippolytus* so the women of Thebes are the pawns of Dionysus in the *Bacchae*. The dramatic action centres on Pentheus' blasphemy and his rejection of Dionysus rather than on the women, who are 'offstage' and merely described by others until Agave's appearance in the final scene. Pentheus makes derogatory remarks about women throughout. His first words in the play are:

> I happened to be abroad, away from this land,
> when I heard of strange evils in this city,
> that our women had left their homes
> and were pretending to be Bacchants,
> and were rushing about in the wooded mountains
> honouring the new god Dionysus – whoever he is – with dances.
> In the middle of the revels stand full wine bowls,
> one then another creeps into a lonely spot
> to serve the lusts of men.
> They say that they are Maenad priestesses,
> but they put Aphrodite before Bacchus.
>
> (215-25)

He ends his speech with the statement:

> Whenever the fruit of the vine is present at a women's feast
> I say that there is nothing wholesome in their revels.
>
> (260-2)

These are the two stock accusations levelled against women in Athenian literature, especially in comedy, that, given the opportunity, women will over-indulge in wine and sex. But Pentheus is certainly not portrayed as an admirable or sympathetic character in this play;

Fig. 10 Maenad, from fifth-century red-figure vase.

his description of the women's activities is proved false by the herds-man's report and Pentheus himself is shown to be a voyeur.

The prophet Teiresias responds to Pentheus' outburst and disputes his view of women:

> Dionysus will not force women to have self-control in sexual matters,
> but self-control is already present in their nature
> in respect of all things...

(314-17)

Pentheus returns to his theme in his first debate with the disguised Dionysus. The god admits that Bacchic rituals are mostly performed at night which prompts Pentheus to assert: 'This leads women to deception and corruption' (487). The Theban women in the *Bacchae* are turned into hunters, and hunters who behave like wild beasts rather than humans, but they act like this because they are in the power of a god. At the end of the play the audience's sympathy is with the women, represented by Agave as she realises the awfulness of what she has done.

In none of these plays did Euripides attack women – the condemnations of women uttered by his characters must be viewed with reference to the characters who express them. Female characters such as Medea and Hecabe (in the play of that name) do commit atrocities, but then so did Aeschylus' Clytemnestra (and no one calls that poet a woman-hater) and so do countless male tragic characters. Medea and Hecabe commit atrocities not because they are women, but as a response to appalling treatment. Their suffering leads to a desire for revenge, a favourite theme of Euripides, and such is human nature that the revenge is often more terrible than the crime which it repays.

The gods

As was noted earlier, Euripides' belief or lack of belief in the gods is a controversial topic.

(a) Medea

No gods are represented on stage in the *Medea* but they are appealed to by almost every character in the play. Medea herself calls on Zeus, Themis, Artemis and Hecate, as well as Helios, her grandfather the Sun; she is also preoccupied with oaths and the betrayal of vows. Hermes, Aphrodite and Apollo are also mentioned by the Chorus. When Aigeus appears on his return (from the Delphic Oracle, no doubts are cast on the veracity of either Apollo or his oracle (unlike Sophocles' *Oedipus Tyrannus*). It is true that Jason is at a loss to understand why the gods do not punish Medea for her crimes but there is no suggestion that the gods do not exist.

(b) Hippolytus

The goddess Aphrodite, not only delivers the prologue but is the motivator of the entire dramatic action of the *Hippolytus* (although the traditional version of the Phaedra legend, that her whole family was cursed by Aphrodite because they were the descendants of Helios who had revealed Aphrodite's infidelity to her husband Hephaistos, is ignored by Euripides). The goddess Artemis appears in the final scene to reconcile Theseus and Hippolytus. In addition to their appearances as characters the two goddesses permeate the entire play as the forces which they represent: Aphrodite as love, passion, emotion and sexual desire; Artemis as chastity, purity, abstinence and self-control. Phaedra is clearly under the domination of Aphrodite, and Hippolytus of Artemis, but both human characters are also seen to be engaged in a conflict between the two opposing forces within themselves.

The role of the gods in the *Hippolytus* has been interpreted in different ways by scholars. Some have suggested that by representing the goddesses as such spiteful and vindictive characters Euripides intended to show that the gods were not worthy of worship. Others argue that it was not the gods themselves which Euripides was criticising but the myths about them and their representation as human beings (anthropomorphic) with human failings (Plato rejected the myths for the same reason in his *Republic*). Another view is that Euripides used gods as symbols, as personifications of abstract psychological forces. It is impossible to know for certain what was in the poet's mind when he wrote his play, but it can be confidently asserted that neither Aphrodite nor Artemis emerges as admirable. The opening lines of Aphrodite's prologue speech were quoted earlier; the tone is consistent throughout. The goddess demands vengeance and mortals, even innocent ones, must suffer: 'My enemies will pay as great a penalty as will satisfy me' (49-50). At the end of the play Artemis is shown to be equally vindictive and scarcely a model of self-restraint:

> Aphrodite's anger will not fall unavenged...
> Whichever mortal proves to be most dear to her,
> I shall take vengeance on him with my own hand,
> with this bow from which none can escape.
>
> (1417-22)

Throughout the play references are made to the gods' vengeful natures and the need for mortals to placate them. In the very first scene a Servant advises Hippolytus not to neglect Aphrodite since gods, like men, hate arrogance and expect their due. When Hippolytus has rejected his advice, the Servant prays to Aphrodite and asks forgiveness for Hippolytus, adding:

> ...he speaks empty words; it seems best not to hear them.
> It is necessary for gods to be wiser than men.
>
> (119-20)

An intentionally ironic comment on the part of the poet, I am sure. However, Aphrodite can be gentle instead of destructive, as the Nurse points out to Phaedra:

> Aphrodite is not to be resisted
> when she rushes in at full force;
> she comes with peace to the one who yields,
> but she seizes any whom she finds excessively arrogant
> and– what do you suppose?– maltreats them.

(443-6)

Poseidon does not appear on stage in the *Hippolytus* but he has a role in the play as the fulfiller of the curse with which Theseus causes his son's death. Again this raises the question of the morality of the gods: should Poseidon have granted Theseus' wish and brought about the death of an innocent youth? Artemis provides the answer:

> The law among the gods is this:
> no one of us is willing to get in the way
> of another's intended purpose,
> but we always stand aside.

(1328-30)

She adds:

> The gods do not rejoice when pious men die;
> but we destroy the wicked
> along with their children and entire house.

(1339-41)

(c) Bacchae

The *Bacchae* deals with a similar topic, this time the vengeance is that of Dionysus. He, too, is shown as capable of both peaceful beneficence and appalling violence. The god describes himself as:

> ...son of Zeus, Dionysus,
> who was the last born of the gods,
> the most terrible and the most gentle to mankind.

(859-61)

This, Euripides' last, play has been interpreted by some as an indication of the poet's religious conversion in old age, and by others, in similar ways to the *Hippolytus*, as a condemnation of myth, or as a symbolic representation of the conflict between inner feelings (in this case civilised against animal and repressed against unrestrained). Unlike the Aphrodite and the Artemis of the earlier play, Dionysus appears as a character throughout the *Bacchae*, although until the final scene he is pretending to be a mortal, a stranger who has come to spread the new cult.

Once again the idea of gods as vengeful beings is stressed. In the first scene Teiresias urges Cadmus on:

> Let us go, Cadmus, and let us intercede
> ...so that the god does not do anything untoward.
>
> (360-3)

At the end of the play Cadmus pleads with Dionysus:

> *Cadmus*: ...you are punishing us too severely.
> *Dionysus*: I, a god, was mocked by you.
> *Cadmus*: It is not right that the gods should match mortals in anger.
>
> (1346-8)

Cadmus' words in this extract are reminiscent of the Servant's at the beginning of the *Hippolytus*.

The whole family of Cadmus is punished harshly, although their attitudes towards the god were different. The women, because they had previously denied the parentage and divinity of Dionysus, were possessed by the god. His power enabled them to effect the miracles described by the Herdsman but it also caused them to kill Pentheus. Agave and her sisters are further punished by the god with exile.

Cadmus appears to have recognised the new god, for he dresses up as a Bacchant and prepares to set off to the mountain with the blind prophet Teiresias. However, when Cadmus is challenged by Pentheus he declares:

> Even if this god is, as you say, not a god,
> let him be called a god by you.
> Tell a noble lie, so that glory may come
> to us and all our family,
> as Semele will seem to have given birth to a god.
> You know the pitiable fate of Actaeon
> whom the flesh-eating hounds, which he had reared himself,
> tore apart in the fields because he had boasted
> that he was better than Artemis at hunting.

So that you do not suffer some such fate,
come here and I will crown your head with ivy;
give the god honour with us.

(333-42)

Cadmus' piety is thus revealed to be nothing more than an insurance
policy, motivated by a desire for glory and a fear of punishment. His
reward is to be turned into a snake, with his wife Harmonia, and to lead
a horde of barbarians against Greek cities.

Pentheus, in spite of the warnings of Cadmus and Teiresias and of
the disguised Dionysus, completely refuses to accept the new god. He
learns nothing from Dionysus' miraculous escape from prison and the
destruction of the palace, nor from the escape of the women prisoners,
nor from the description of the miracles performed by the women on the
mountain. However, Pentheus is not an atheist; he recognises the power
of Zeus and sincerely believes that Semele was punished by Zeus for
blasphemy:

This man says that Dionysus is a god,
that he was once sewn into the thigh of Zeus,
but he was burnt with lightning flames along with his mother,
because she lied about her mating with Zeus.
Is this not deserving of a terrible death by hanging –
for uttering such blasphemous insults...?

(242-7)

There is, of course, irony here, since it is Pentheus who is blaspheming,
but the quotation also serves to illustrate the limits of his disbelief. His
refusal to worship Dionysus, especially the Dionysus presented by the
perfumed, smiling, long-haired stranger, is very similar to Hippolytus'
exclusion of Aphrodite. Both are afraid of the unrestrained and the
sexual, as is shown by Pentheus' attitude to women and his voyeuristic
desire to see them drunk and making love.

Teiresias, the old blind prophet, is the only character (excluding
the Chorus) in the *Bacchae* who is not punished by the god. He speaks
out firmly against those who apply rationalism or sophistry to religion:

We do not talk cleverly about the gods.
We hold the traditions of our fathers which are as old as time,
no logical argument will throw them down,
not even if wisdom is found in the keenest of minds.

(200-3)

He then describes how the legend about Dionysus being sewn up in Zeus' thigh originated because of confusion with the Greek word for 'hostage', but he does not provide a rational explanation (286-97). Teiresias replaces one myth with another and he is the only character who comes out of the play well; there is no sign of Euripides the atheist or pupil of the sophists here.

The Chorus similarly support Dionysus throughout, even to the extent of rejoicing at the murder of Pentheus. Their odes are some of the longest in Euripides' extant tragedies and they all have the theme of the power and greatness of the god. Did Euripides intend this chorus of foreign Bacchants to direct the sympathies of the audience towards the god? Surely the audience would have been horrified and revolted by the delusion and death of Pentheus? Dionysus is portrayed as a creator and a destroyer: was the play intended to celebrate the god's divinity or to condemn the orgiastic, violent nature of some Bacchic worship?

(d) Divine resolutions

All three of the plays which I have examined include a divine (or in the case of *Medea* semi-divine) denouement or resolution. Each not only brings the play to a conclusion by explaining the reasons behind the tragic action, but also links the drama to some cult practice or myth well-known to the audience. Medea, in her chariot of the Sun with the bodies of her children is a virtual *deus ex machina*. Her statement about burying the children in the holy precinct of Acraea fits with contemporary belief and cult practice. She also predicts Jason's legendary ignominious death, struck on the head by a timber from the *Argo*. At the end of the *Hippolytus*, Artemis announces that young girls will cut locks of their hair in honour of Hippolytus on their wedding night (not an especially appropriate honour for the anti-marriage Hippolytus!) and that Phaedra will be celebrated in songs. Dionysus, as we have seen, decrees the fates of Cadmus, his wife and daughters, connecting Cadmus and Harmonia to the legend of the Encheleis. This underlining of the outcome of the play by a god has been regarded by some commentators as a Euripidean innovation but Athene had played a similar role in Aeschylus' *Eumenides* and Hermes in his *Prometheus Bound*, although neither arrived unexpectedly on the crane. These same plays by Aeschylus disprove another assertion sometimes made about Euripides: that he was the first to portray gods as characters on the stage.

Whether these gods were created by a rationalist or by a believer will remain a topic of controversy. Did Euripides depict them as such powerful and vindictive beings in order to warn men that they must worship the gods or face the consequences (an idea put forward in one of the choral odes of his *Electra*)? Or was he saying that gods as petty and vengeful as this cannot exist? Or was he merely doing his best as a playwright to present dramatic and exciting versions of the myths? There are no simple answers to these questions, but perhaps Euripides did not intend there to be.

Heroic or unheroic?

In Aristophanes' *Frogs* Euripides was accused of portraying common characters in his tragedies rather than the virtuous martial heroes which Aeschylus claimed were to be found in his plays. He was also mocked for dressing his heroes in rags, a point discussed at the beginning of this chapter. Aristotle (*Poetics*, 1460b33) quoted a saying of Sophocles: 'I portray men as they should be, Euripides as they are.' Modern scholars have written much about Euripides' 'realism': Professor Knox (in his article on Euripides in the *Cambridge History of Classical Literature*) asserts: 'The disturbance of the heroic atmosphere by realistic scenes which may even verge on the comic is constant . . . ' and Vellacott has written: ' . . . how frequently Euripides takes familiar heroic characters, identifies them with his fellow-Athenians in contemporary situations, and presents them acting in embarrassing or disgraceful ways, at the same time showing that these are the accepted ways of his own society.'

To deal first with the topic of common characters, it is true that the *Medea* begins with a nurse and a tutor, but nurses and tutors also appear in plays by Aeschylus and Sophocles and the Nurse Cilissa in Aeschylus' *Choephoroi* is a very down-to-earth character. There are a Servant and a Nurse in the *Hippolytus* and a Herdsman in the *Bacchae*; but Aeschylus began his *Agamemnon* with a Watch- man's speech and a Herdsman has a vital role in Sophocles' *Oedipus Tyrannus*. The marriage of Electra to a poor Mycenaean peasant was a startling Euripidean innovation, but that will be discussed in Chapter 6.

More interesting is the point made by Vellacott, that Euripides showed traditional heroes in an unheroic light. Jason is a good example of this; his attitude to Medea is patronising and insensitive, he is only interested in obtaining security for himself and he equates that security with a fixed home, wealth and an appropriate marriage. He is far removed from the gallant and adventurous leader of the Argonauts. Medea condemns him bitterly at their first encounter:

> I have a wonderful husband in you,
> and a faithful one, poor wretch that I am!
> I shall flee this land, cast out as an exile,
> without any friends, alone with my abandoned children–
> a fine disgrace for a new bridegroom!
> I, the one who saved your life,
> and your children wandering as beggars!
> O Zeus, why have you provided clear signs for men
> to tell what is counterfeit from what is pure gold,
> but when it is necessary to know clearly an evil man
> there is no distinguishing mark bred into his body?
>
> (*Medea* 510-19)

Jason has no creditable case to make in reply; he claims that he had married the king's daughter not because he was tired of Medea and wanted a new wife, nor because he wanted more children but:

> ...so that we might live well, the most important thing,
> and not want for anything;
> I know that everyone shuns a poor man
> and friends keep out of his way...
>
> (559-61)

Some of the Athenian male audience may have sympathised with Jason in his desire for comfort and prosperity, but nowhere in the play can his conduct or speech be described as truly noble or heroic. On the other hand, Sophocles presents a most unheroic Odysseus in his *Philoctetes* and the Agamemnon of Aeschylus' tragedy does not seem especially admirable as he yields to his wife's flattery and steps on to the tapestries.

A sentiment similar to that expressed by Medea about recognising men's true natures is found in the *Hippolytus*. Ironically, the words are spoken by Theseus who is himself so mistaken about the truth:

> Alas, there should exist for mortals some clear sign
> as to who are their friends, ·
> and a means of distinguishing between men's minds,
> so as to know who is a true friend and who is not.

All men should have two voices,
the one honest and the other however it might be,
so that the one which was involved in evil
might be refuted by the just one
and we would not be deceived.

(*Hippolytus* 925-31)

From this we might infer that morality was of some concern to Euripides
and that he did not portray ignoble characters as examples to be followed
but rather to be avoided.

Although Medea and her schemes are hardly to be admired she is
cast in a 'heroic' mould. She steels herself to commit inhuman deeds in
order to gain vengeance and to prevent herself from being laughed at by
her enemies (an anxiety which preoccupies her e.g. *Medea* 383, 797 &
1049). But at the same time she is portrayed as a woman with realistic
maternal instincts. In her famous monologue (1019-80) in which she
appears to change her mind four times, she speaks of the softness of
children's skin, the sweetness of their breath and how she will not see
their brides or their wedding days. Medea's quarrels with Jason and his
taunts about her sexual jealousy might also be regarded as signs of
'realism'– but are these any more true to life than the quarrel between
Electra and her mother in Sophocles' *Electra*? With such a small
proportion of each poet's plays surviving it is difficult to make an
accurate assessment. Certainly we shall see in the next chapter that
Euripides portrayed a very down-to-earth Electra and an unheroic
Orestes in his version of *Electra*.

Language and structure

It was not only Euripides' characters who were mocked in Aristophanes'
Frogs for being common but also his language. On the other hand,
Aristotle (*Rhetoric*, 1404b5) praised Euripides for introducing words
from everyday speech into his tragedies. In fact Euripides skilfully
adapted the tragic metre, iambic trimeter, so that his dialogue more
accurately reflected the rhythms of normal speech and his characters of
every social class use colloquialisms.

Euripides' longer speeches, referred to by some commentators as
rhesis, reflect the dominance of rhetoric in the People's Assembly and
the lawcourts of Athens at the time. Characters employ logic and almost
engage in formal debate. Phaedra's speech about morals sounds more
like oratory than the words of a woman overwhelmed by love:

> ...I have often considered in the long hours of the night
> how the lives of some mortals are ruined.
> They do not seem to me to do things which are rather wicked
> because of some natural inclination,
> For most people are right-minded.
> but consider it in this way:
> we understand and know what is good
> but we do not do it,
> some of us because of laziness
> and some preferring some other pleasure
> instead of goodness...

(*Hippolytus* 375-83)

In the same play Hippolytus begins his defence to Theseus in a very formal fashion, similar in style to Socrates in Plato's *Apology*:

> I am unaccustomed to making a speech in front of a crowd,
> but I am more skilled at speaking
> in front of a small number of my friends of my own age.
> This is natural; for those who are fools among wise men
> can speak and seem more intelligent in front of crowds...

(986-9)

Again, a similar style is to be found in some of Sophocles' plays: for example Electra's debate with Clytemnestra. But the two poets were contemporaries and were exposed to the same rhetorical influences as well as to one another's.

The inclusion of everyday language does not mean that Euripides' poetry is devoid of richness and imagery. The American Professor Charles Segal has written at length on the images of the sea in the *Hippolytus* and many commentators have pointed out the recurrent animal and hunting images inthe *Bacchae*. For example, Dionysus is referred to as a bull, a serpent and a lion and he appears to Pentheus as a bull when the young king tries to imprison him. Pentheus himself is described as the young of a lioness and Agave mistakes him for a lion when she kills him and brings his head back to Thebes. The *Medea* contains much nautical imagery.

Like Sophocles, Euripides made use of word-play and irony. In the *Bacchae* there is a pun on Pentheus' name since the Greek *penthos* means sorrow. The fact that Dionysus is disguised as a human provides many opportunities for dramatic irony when the god confronts Pentheus:

Pentheus: Next, give up this thyrsus from your hands.
Dionysus: Take it from me yourself. I am carrying the thyrsus
of Dionysus.
Pentheus: We shall keep guard on your body in prison.
Dionysus: The god himself will release me, whenever I wish.

....

Dionysus: He is present now and sees what I am suffering.
Pentheus: Where is he? He is not clear to my eyes.

(495-501)

A series of double meanings occurs later as Dionysus leads
Pentheus to his death:

Dionysus: You alone are suffering for this city, you alone.
The struggles which were fated for you are waiting.
Follow. I go as your escort and saviour,
another will bring you back here.
Pentheus: My mother?
Dionysus: You will be an example to all...
Pentheus: It is for this I go.
Dionysus: You will return being carried...
Pentheus: You speak of my being spoiled.
Dionysus: In the hands of your mother.

(963-9)

Euripides developed irony still further in the depiction of total role
reversals. In the *Bacchae* Pentheus starts out determined to assert his
masculine authority over what he sees as weak and deluded women;
he is equally determined to dominate Dionysus, the effeminate
stranger and he casts himself in the role of hunter. At the end of the
play Pentheus himself is deluded; he becomes the victim of both the
women and Dionysus; instead of being a hunter he becomes the
hunted, the prey of others. In the first scene he was scornful of
Teiresias and Cadmus for wearing the insignia of Bacchants, yet he
goes to his death not only dressed as a Bacchant but also as a woman.

There is balance and reversal, too, in complete scenes within
Euripides' tragedies. In the *Bacchae* Dionysus' gradual filling of
Pentheus' mind with madness can be seen as parallel to the final scene
in which Cadmus slowly clears Agave's mind of delusion. In the *Medea*
the first encounter between Jason and Medea is balanced by their final
meeting. In the one Medea is emotional, Jason cool and in control; in the
other, Jason is reduced to pleading and abuse while Medea remains

aloof, unmoved and totally in charge of the situation. The characters of Phaedra and Hippolytus are a pair. Phaedra has been overcome by Aphrodite, by love and passion, yet she is initially determined to master it by self-control and then to die honourably and with a clear conscience. Hippolytus claims to be a model of self-control but his response to the Nurse's revelation is a far from restrained outburst and he faces death filled with excessive self-pity. Professor Charles Segal has pointed out the parallels, in language and in action, between the scene in which Phaedra is carried in on a bed, weak and longing for death, and that in which Hippolytus, mangled and near to death, is brought on by his companions. Euripides was obviously a craftsman who devoted much thought to the structure of his plays.

The role of the chorus

Professor Erich Segal (in his essay *Euripides: Poet of Paradox*) wrote: 'It is also true that Euripides banished choral drama from the stage. His 'intrigue' plays made the chorus seem very much out of place. Fifteen Ideal Spectators may look well in a palace, but they considerably clutter up a living room ... Time and again his choruses are cautioned to keep secrets that they have overheard; it becomes increasingly clear that they should not be there in the first place ... ' This does not seem to apply to the three plays which I have been considering. The Chorus of Corinthian Women in the *Medea* have already been discussed in the section about women. They are certainly involved in the play, particularly in their role as 'sounding board' for Medea, and their odes are closely connected to the dramatic action. The choice of Corinthian Women for the role is a good one as they can accentuate Medea's status and isolation as a foreigner. Medea herself refers to the difference between them:

> But the same argument does not apply to you and me,
> for this is your city and the home of your fathers
> and you have a pleasant life and the company of friends.
> But I am alone, without a city ...

(252-5)

Once Medea has announced her plan to kill the children the Chorus make a positive attempt to dissuade her. Medea ignores their request; but they do not withdraw their support from her. Even when the Messenger reports the horrible death of the princess the Chorus do not appear shocked but comment:

On this day divine power seems to touch Jason
justly with many disasters.

(1231-2)

It is only when Medea actually murders the children that the Corinthian
Women cease to take her side. Was Euripides using the Chorus to present
his own views to the audience or merely to propose an alternative to
outright condemnation of Medea? The Athenian audience might have
expected guidance from the chorus in a tragedy and, at the very least,
the Corinthian Women's open support for Medea may have caused them
to hesitate before condemning her totally.

The words with which the Chorus end this play are controversial
because, with the addition of one other line, they appear as the closing
verses of four other extant plays by Euripides – *Alcestis, Andromache,
Helen* and the *Bacchae*. Is this the result of a later copyist's error or was
Euripides intentionally being trite? The lines themselves certainly imply
a belief in divine providence:

Zeus on Olympus is dispensor of many fates;
the gods accomplish many things which are not expected
and the things which were expected did not happen.
The god found a way for what was not expected.
In such a way this affair turned out.

(1415-19)

The Chorus of Troezenian Women in the *Hippolytus* are similarly
sympathetic to Phaedra. But in this play the audience knows something
which the Chorus do not, namely that Phaedra is merely the tool of
Aphrodite in her plan for vengeance on Hippolytus. Like the Chorus in
Aeschylus' *Agamemnon*, the women decide not to intervene when cries
for help are herad from within the palace after Phaedra has committed
suicide. Professor Kitto suggested that Euripides purposely made the
Chorus stand aside and be a little remote from the action, so as not to
obscure the audience's 'vision of the inner drama'. Certainly their ode
which precedes Phaedra's death begins with the idea 'O, that I might
be...somewhere else' (*Hippolytus* 732-51).

The Chorus in the *Bacchae* have a much larger part, but they are
curiously detached from the actual plot. It is the women of Thebes, the
Maenads who are not seen on stage, whose miraculous actions are
reported by the herdsman and who eventually kill Pentheus. The Bacchants of the Chorus are foreign women, they have come to Thebes with
Dionysus but believe that he is a human follower rather than the god

himself (once again the audience knows more than the Chorus). They are unswerving in their support of Dionysus, but they are most memorable for the vigour and rhythmic excitement of their odes which create the atmosphere of the play and illustrate well the power of the god.

Conclusion

Fifteen of Euripides' surviving plays were presented during the Peloponnesian War. Modern critics have often identified 'anti-war' propaganda within them. Certainly in the *Suppliant Women* there are images of the insanity of war and in the *Andromache, Hecabe, Trojan Women* and *Iphigenia in Aulis* much sympathy is aroused for captive women and for parents who lose their sons in war. But such themes were not new, the same ideas had been expressed forcefully in Aeschylus' *Agamemnon* in 458 BC by the Herald, Clytemnestra and Cassandra and in a choral ode.

What was a Euripidean innovation was the development of the melodrama, tragi-comedy or happy-ending play. In some of his tragedies the solution seems to be more in human hands and tragedy is not inevitable. The *Alcestis*, which Euripides presented in place of a satyr play in 438 BC, is a forerunner of this type. Alcestis, the faithful young wife, is rescued from death by Heracles and what was a funeral becomes a celebration of life. Such last minute escapes, as a result of a fortuitous recognition or the intervention of a god, occur in the *Ion* and the *Iphigenia in Tauris*. The arrival of the Athenian king Aigeus in the *Medea*, which Aristotle described as *alogon* (absurd), similarly serves to provide an unexpected place of escape for Medea, but hardly leads to a happy ending for the play.

In that same play, while cunningly feigning submission to Creon, Medea lamented her 'reputation', commenting:

No sensible man should ever bring up his children
by having them taught to be excessively clever...
they incur unfortunate envy from their fellow citizens.
To the stupid you seem useless,
introducing strange cleverness rather than wisdom.
But you will be regarded by those who believe
that they themselves have subtle knowledge
as something offensive to the city.
I myself share in this misfortune.
For I am clever and am envied by some...

(294-304)

These lines are well-suited to Medea's argument and her predicament at that moment. They also serve to illustrate the diversity of opinions amongst Euripidean scholars. They have been interpreted as both a direct reference to Socrates and as an expression of the poet's own feelings, that as a 'clever' man he was mistrusted and misunderstood.

By presenting his audience with the innermost thoughts, self-examination and motivation of his characters Euripides made it difficult wholly to condemn or to praise them. As we have seen neither Medea nor Jason is completely admirable and the same is true of Phaedra and Hippolytus, and of Pentheus and Dionysus. Those who liked a message or a moral to be clearly spelt out would have found little satisfaction in Euripides' plays. However, there is no denying his greatness as a poet, his brilliance in depicting the human spirit in suffering and torment, and his ability to present more than one side of a dilemma. His influence on later playwrights such as Menander (and through him Plautus and Terence) and Seneca is well documented. What most Athenians really thought about him is unlikely ever to be accurately known, but Plutarch in his *Life of Nicias* recounts how knowledge of Euripides' plays saved the lives of some Athenians after the defeat in Sicily in 413 BC:

> They say that many of those who were saved and came home greeted Euripides with affection. They described how some had been set free from slavery for reciting as many of his verses as they remembered and how others, wandering about after the battle, received food and drink for singing some of his odes.
>
> (XXIX,3)

Clearly parts of his plays were considered to be worth memorising by at least some of the citizens and the Sicilians were exceptionally eager to hear them.

Chapter 6
Three Versions of the Electra Story

The treatment of the same episode by each of the three tragedians illustrates clearly how they used myth as a springboard for their art rather than as a straitjacket. Aeschylus had presented the *Libation Bearers* as the second play of his *Oresteia* trilogy in 458 BC. Both Sophocles and Euripides chose to deal with the same theme in a single play, each now known as *Electra*. Critics are divided as to which was produced first, but it is generally agreed that both were produced in the period 420-410 BC. There seems to have been a revival of Aeschylus' *Oresteia* in c. 424 BC and his version would undoubtedly have been in the minds of the younger poets and of many of their audience. Euripides' *Electra* is certainly unorthodox and it has been regarded by many as a parody of Aeschylus' version; Sophocles' play is then seen as a later response in an attempt to redress the balance. Other commentators have suggested that Euripides was merely restating Aeschylus' moral message more clearly – believing that the *Oresteia* was a subtle condemnation of the matricide, the acquittal of Orestes and the defeat of the Furies. Certainly echoes of and allusions to the *Oresteia* can be identified in the *Electra* of both Sophocles and Euripides.

My intention in this final chapter is to examine some aspects of the three poets' treatment of the Electra story, highlighting their differences and similarities. Obviously Sophocles and Euripides had to choose a narrower focus for their versions as single plays than Aeschylus, who, as we saw in Chapter 3, was able to develop themes and ideas throughout the whole trilogy. However, the *Libation Bearers* and both *Electras* concern the events of a single day, encompassing the return of Orestes prompted by Apollo, his reunion with Electra and the killing of Clytemnestra and Aegisthus. In Sophocles' version the story is presented with little criticism or judgement and the actions and emotions of the human characters are explored more than divine will or the inexorability of the cycle of vengeance. Electra herself is the main focus of the play: she is on stage for nine-tenths of it and has one of the longest speaking parts in extant Greek tragedy. At the same time new characters, the sister Chrysothemis and the old Tutor, are introduced and a more complex sub-plot is developed. Euripides reduced the story to a much less heroic level: the palace setting is replaced by a peasant's hut, Electra has been married to an aging peasant and Orestes has crept over the border into Argos, prepared to flee if anyone should recognise him and with no clear idea of how to carry out his vengeance.

Scene setting

The prologue of Aeschylus' *Libation Bearers* is unfortunately not preserved in its entirety; parts of it have been pieced together from fragments surviving in other sources. Orestes, accompanied by the silent Pylades, has arrived at his father's tomb. He prays to Hermes for support, leaves a lock of his hair as an offering, and hides when he sees Electra and the Chorus of slave women approaching. The Chorus' initial ode introduces the theme of the blood pollution on the House and the 'godless woman' who murdered her husband. Electra is seen to be diffident as she asks the Chorus for advice about how to present the offerings which her mother has sent. It is the Chorus who suggest praying for Orestes' return and vengeance. Electra does so, at the same time making known her situation as a slave to her mother. Finally she notices the lock of hair.

Sophocles' play begins with virtually two separate prologues, one male, the other female. The Tutor is the first to speak; he sets the scene and introduces Orestes and Pylades. Orestes then outlines the plot which has been prepared, the false report of his death and the arrival of the urn. Electra is heard grieving inside the palace and Orestes wants to listen, but the Tutor despatches him to make offerings at his father's grave. Electra appears and sings a long ode about her father's murder and her own sorrows, calling on Hades, Hermes, Persephone and the Furies to help her gain revenge and to send her brother home. The Chorus of slave women have no formal entry ode, but they join in a lyric exchange with Electra. They criticise her excessive grief and point out that she has two sisters, Chrysothemis and Iphianassa, who do not grieve as she does. Electra's complaints about her treatment are interrupted by the arrival of Chrysothemis, who is on her way to Agamemnon's tomb with offerings from their mother. Electra herself does not visit her father's tomb and the meeting with the disguised Orestes does not take place until line 1098.

Fig. 11 Orestes at the tomb of Agamemnon, from a relief in the Louvre.

Many scholars have commented upon the contrast drawn between Orestes and Electra in these opening scenes – the one a man of practical planning and action who uses the rational language of public life, and the other an irrational, frenzied creature, filled with self-pity and despair and given to emotional outpourings.

It is the old Peasant, husband of Electra, whom Euripides chose to deliver his prologue. He sets the scene and describes Agamemnon's murder. Unusually for a Euripidean prologue the speaker does not identify himself at first; it is not until line 35 that the Peasant explains who he is, after mentioning Aegisthus' fear that Electra would bear a noble son who might overthrow him. The Peasant also refers to Orestes, but in the context of wondering how he would feel about his sister's marriage if he ever returned home. Electra arrives carrying her water jar and insists that she must carry out menial household tasks herself. After the couple have gone their separate ways, Orestes and Pylades appear and Orestes states that he has come at Apollo's command to avenge his father's murder. He has already sacrificed at his father's tomb and he has now come to find his sister whom he knows to be living nearby. When Electra re-appears with her water jar Orestes mistakes her for a servant and hides. The Chorus enters and they sing a lyric exchange with Electra about the festival of Hera. In keeping with her pessimistic outlook, when Electra finally notices Orestes and Pylades she assumes that they are wicked men intent upon harming her.

Within the first two hundred lines each poet has set out the main themes and characters of his play. In each case Orestes has appeared in person and announced his purpose and, quite independently, someone else has referred to Orestes and the possibility of his return. Electra's character and circumstances have also been firmly established. Sophocles' innovations of the old Tutor, the urn and the compliant sister Chrysothemis as a foil to Electra have been well signposted. Similarly, Electra's strange marriage and the rather unheroic nature of Orestes and Electra are quickly revealed to the audience by Euripides.

The recognition scenes

Recognition scenes (*anagnoriseis*) are an intrinsic part of the tradition of Greek myths and legends. In Homer's *Odyssey* the old nurse Eurycleia recognises the disguised Odysseus by a scar (XIX, 467ff.) and, later, Odysseus offers the 'token' of the shared secret of the structure of their bed to his wife Penelope when she refuses to recognise him (XXIII, 179). In the *Libation Bearers* Electra is at Agamemnon's tomb when she sees the lock of hair. She tells the Chorus that it is identical to hers and they suggest that it must belong to Orestes (167-78). Electra instantly concludes that he must have sent the hair because he would not have dared to have come himself, but then she suggests that perhaps it is not Orestes' hair after all. It is at that moment that she sees the footprints and she proceeds to assert that they match hers exactly:

> The heels and the outlines of the tendons
> measured against my footprints are just the same.

(209-10)

Orestes himself appears as she speaks, but his words are circumspect and she does not immediately grasp his identity:

> *Orestes:* You have come into the sight of what you have for a long time been praying for.
> *Electra:* You know which man I was naming?
> *Orestes:* I know that you have been longing for Orestes very much.
> *Electra:* And in what way have I good fortune in my prayers?
> *Orestes:* I am he. Do not search for anyone closer to you than I am.
> *Electra:* But, stranger, surely you are weaving some trap round me?
> *Orestes:* Then I am forming plots against myself.
> *Electra:* But you are wanting to mock me in the middle of my troubles?
> *Orestes:* I would be mocking my own troubles if I were mocking yours.
> *Electra:* Shall I call you Orestes...

(215-24)

Electra is finally convinced when Orestes produces a piece of patterned cloth which she herself had woven and which presumably he had taken into exile with him. After the initial hasty jumping to conclusions the actual recognition process is a slow and unconfident one.

Euripides introduced all of these tokens into his recognition scene, but they are suggested by the old Servant (who has been to the tomb) and rejected scornfully by Electra as being ridiculous. The old Servant first mentions the lock of hair and tells her to compare it with her own to see if the colours match. Electra replies that the hair of a young nobleman would not be like a woman's and that many people who are not related by blood share the same colour hair. Next, the old man speaks of a footprint which may match hers. Electra is scathing: how could a print have been made in rocky ground and surely a man's foot would be bigger than a woman's? Finally, the old Servant asks whether there might not be a piece of cloth which Electra had woven for Orestes before he went away by which he might be recognised. Electra retorts that she was only a child at the time and even if she had known how to weave clothing it is unlikely that Orestes would still be wearing it now, unless it had somehow grown larger as he did! This passage has caused much controversy: clearly Euripides was in some way mocking Aeschylus' recognition scene. However, some critics have regarded the whole scene as a later interpolation, while others have gone to extraordinary lengths to defend Aeschylus (for example, arguing that brother and sister shared some idiosyncratic foot formation). More recent commentators have suggested that Euripides was playing some sort of literary, theatrical game with the stock recognition scene and was showing his awareness of his own place within the tragic genre. There is irony in Electra's rational objections, because the old man has correctly read the signs of Orestes' presence and she has not. Indeed it is this same old man, a faithful servant of Agamemnon who had smuggled Orestes out of the country, who actually recognises Orestes in person. He examines Orestes closely, fairly certain that it is he and then notices the scar on his brow to confirm this belief. Electra is only then convinced.

In Sophocles' version it is Chrysothemis, the acquiescent sister, who visits their father's tomb and finds newly poured libations and a lock of hair. She rushes back triumphantly to Electra but her joy is shortlived; Electra has just heard the Tutor's false story of Orestes' death and she is convinced that the offerings were made in memory of Orestes rather than by him. Electra is later confronted by Orestes, disguised as a Phocian, bringing the urn supposedly containing Orestes' ashes. Her grief is so great that Orestes cannot bear to deceive her and he proves his identity by producing his father's seal ring. This is probably the most convincing proof of the three. However, once Electra's laments have been excluded, Sophocles' recognition scene is by far the shortest and least developed. It includes no initial uncertainty or rejection; these emotions had already been expressed in the scene with Chrysothemis.

Aeschylus showed an Electra filled with irrational and dramatic imaginings, who wanted to believe in Orestes' return and then lost confidence. Euripides' scene was more disturbing in its rejection of the traditional tokens and the introduction of the scar. Sophocles almost underplays the recognition scene: his interest seems to have been more in Electra's sufferings and emotions in response to the false death report, and in Orestes' reaction to them.

The murders

In the *Libation Bearers* Orestes and Pylades gain entry to the palace disguised as strangers bringing news of Orestes' death. Aegisthus arrives later, unarmed because of the old nurse Cilissa's false message, and he is killed first. His cries are heard from within the house.

When Clytemnestra realises what has happened she calls for 'an axe with which to kill a man' (889), obviously intending to strike Orestes. But Orestes arrives before the axe and Clytemnestra has to use persuasion in an effort to escape her fate. She asks for reverence (not pity, a common mistranslation) for the breast which suckled him and finally threatens her son with pursuit by the Furies. When Orestes hesitates, Pylades speaks his only lines of the play and reminds him of Apollo's command. Clytemnestra is taken inside to meet her death and no offstage cries are heard.

Sophocles' Orestes and Pylades are also disguised as Phocian strangers but they bring an urn rather than just a story. The story has been told in dramatic and vivid detail in advance by the old Tutor: Orestes had been 'killed' in a chariot race at the Pythian games, held in honour of Apollo at Delphi. The link with Apollo's oracle is clear but one might also wonder whether the tale was inspired by Orestes' line in the *Libation Bearers*: '...as if I were driving a chariot with horses swerving out of the track...' (1022). Orestes enters the palace with the urn while Electra keeps watch for Aegisthus outside. There is no scene shown between Orestes and Clytemnestra. She is murdered first and her cries are heard from offstage while Electra is rejoicing in front of the doors. Clytemnestra is given only one pleading sentence: 'My son, my son, pity the woman who gave you birth' (*Electra* 1410). Aegisthus' death scene is more dramatic: Sophocles uses a visual effect – a covered corpse is displayed as if it were that of Orestes. The unwitting victim triumphantly and ironically declares:

> O Zeus, I see the body of one who has been destroyed
> by divine displeasure...
>
> (1466-7)

He is soon disabused of his mistake. Aegisthus requests an opportunity to speak in his own defence but Electra urges her brother to kill him at once. The play ends as he is led away.

In both Aeschylus' and Sophocles' versions the murders are committed within the last two hundred lines of the play. Euripides' Aegisthus is killed when the drama has half its course to run. Orestes himself had had no clear plan; it was the old Servant who suggested how Aegisthus might best be murdered. As in several other of Euripides' plays there are strong overtones of ritual sacrifice – Aegisthus is killed while he is actually sacrificing to the Nymphs and the murder weapon is a sacrificial knife. Aegisthus had noticed Orestes and Pylades passing by while he was preparing for the ceremony and he had politely invited them to be his guests; he then asked Orestes to cut up the victim so that the entrails might be examined. He died without discovering who his murderer was, struck from behind by a man who claimed to be a Thessalian stranger. Hardly a heroic act of vengeance!

Electra takes delight in planning Clytemnestra's murder. She summons her to the hut on the pretext that she had given birth to a son ten days before and did not know how to perform the necessary sacrifice of thanksgiving and purification. Mother and daughter engage in a long debate about the justice of Agamemnon's murder before they enter the hut (Sophocles had included a debate on the same theme in an earlier scene of his play). Clytemnestra's cries are heard offstage, the murder is quickly completed and the audience's attention is at once transferred to the children's shame and guilt.

Reactions to the murders

Orestes, in the *Libation Bearers*, makes a speech standing over the corpses of Clytemnestra and Aegisthus. He displays the robe in which Agamemnon had been entangled and calls on Helios, the Sun, as his witness: '...that I carried out this murder with justice' (988) and he repeats that he was obeying Apollo's orders. The Chorus agree that what Orestes did was well done. Scarcely have they spoken when the Furies appear to Orestes and he sets off for Delphi. The resolution comes in the final part of the trilogy.

Critics have differed in their interpretations of the ending of Sophocles' *Electra*. When Orestes appears briefly after the death of Clytemnestra the Chorus find no fault with him: 'His bloody hand is dripping from his sacrifice to Ares; but I cannot blame him' (1422). As in Aeschylus' play, Orestes immediately refers to Apollo's oracle as his motivator. After Aegisthus has been led away the Chorus close the play:

> O family of Atreus, so at last after suffering many evils
> you have come out with difficulty into freedom
> and have gained prosperity through this day's enterprise.
>
> (1508-10)

There is no reference to Orestes' pursuit by the Furies, but the legend was well known to the audience and we should not assume that Sophocles was seeking to alter it. There are certainly references to the Furies at other points in the play and Sophocles has made no attempt to deny their traditional role as avengers. He has merely chosen to present one episode from the story and has focused far more on Electra than on Orestes.

Euripides devoted the last two hundred lines of his play to the aftermath of the murders and their effect upon Orestes and Electra. As soon as the brother and sister appear from killing Clytemnestra they acknowledge that they have done wrong. Orestes calls it a bloody and horrible deed and speaks of his suffering; Electra says that the blame is hers. Orestes recalls that Apollo had instructed him to commit the deed but wonders what country or friend will accept him now – as a matricide. Electra too believes that she will be stateless and will never find the noble husband for whom she has longed. The scene which Aeschylus had partly shown on stage is graphically reported by Orestes: how his mother had bared her breast to him, clung to his neck, touched his cheek and begged for mercy from her child. The account is made more terrible by Orestes' horror as he describes the scene. He had had to cover his eyes with his cloak in order to strike the deadly blow.

In true Euripidean fashion a relief from all this torment is presented by the intervention of the gods. Castor and Polydeuces, the heavenly twins and brothers of Clytemnestra, appear from the crane on the stage roof. They announce that Clytemnestra met a just fate but that Apollo did not give Orestes wise advice. He must now leave Argos and he will be pursued by the Furies until eventually his case is judged by the Areopagus Court. The transformation of the Furies is also prophesied and the entire action of Aeschylus' *Eumenides* is encompassed in a few lines. But that is not all; we are also told that Helen had never really gone to Troy, that Orestes will found a city in Arcadia, that Pylades will marry Electra and take her to Phocis and that the old Peasant will go with them and be made wealthy. The play finishes on a note of mixed relief and sorrow, as brother and sister part so soon after their reunion. Euripides certainly did not leave any loose ends!

Portrayals of Electra and Clytemnestra

(a) Aeschylus

Aeschylus' Electra is diffident at first and, as was noted above, asks advice from the Chorus. Her criticism of Clytemnestra gradually increases and she becomes more vituperative once Orestes has revealed himself to her. The Chorus, Electra and Orestes sing a *kommos* which builds up the tension, invoking the spirits of the dead and referring to Clytemnestra as a cruel viper. The Queen seems to be the strong character portrayed in the *Agamemnon* until we are told by the Chorus of her dream and the terror that it caused. Electra disappears from the play at this point and there is no scene between mother and daughter. Clytemnestra first appears in person to meet Orestes and Pylades, the Phocian strangers, with news of Orestes' death. As was stated in Chapter 3, she greets them cordially and even shows some grief at the news, although the old nurse Cilissa later says that she was only pretending. Once she has realised who Orestes is she argues logically with him, referring to Agamemnon's guilt and the curse to follow. Her final words are: 'This is the snake I gave birth to and suckled' (*Libation Bearers* 928). She does not plead for mercy, but recognises the meaning of her dream and accepts her fate.

(b) Sophocles

Electra is the dominant character in Sophocles' play. She is a character of words; she has more lyrics than any other Sophoclean character and she shows enormous depths of emotions, displaying immoderation in hatred, sorrow and joy. Her excessive grief is commented on by the Chorus in their opening speech and later by Chrysothemis and Clytemnestra. Chrysothemis is used as a foil for Electra, in a somewhat similar way to Ismene in the *Antigone*. Some critics have commented on how harshly Electra treats Chrysothemis, but Chrysothemis, who opens the exchange, adopts quite an accusatory tone:

> What story are you telling now, sister,
> once again having come here outside the door?
> Are you not willing to learn after all this time
> not to give in to your pointless anger?
>
> (328-31)

However, she tempers this immediately by adding that she would defy Clytemnestra and Aegisthus if she had the strength, and by admitting that Electra has justice on her side. Electra responds with taunts about Chrysothemis' cooperation with her father's murderers and her sister's enjoyment of privileges, sumptuous meals and a life of luxury. All these points provide a sharp contrast with Electra's own wretched existence. The two sisters are reconciled when Electra hears of Clytemnestra's dream (this time of Agamemnon's sceptre sprouting into a tree which overshadowed Mycenae), and Electra persuades her sister to take simple offerings from them both to their father's grave. Chrysothemis' joy at finding Orestes' offerings is easily crushed by Electra's sorrow at the false news of Orestes' death. When Electra conceives a plan for the two of them to murder Aegisthus, Chrysothemis refuses to participate and the Chorus support her. Electra is shown to be an extremist.

Sophocles' audience first hear of Clytemnestra from Electra who refers to her mother and her 'bed-partner' splitting Agamemnon's skull with an axe like woodcutters cleaving an oak. This is a violent and dramatic image which is clearly designed to shock. The opening lyrics of the Chorus refer to the Queen's treachery and deceitfulness. However, the most powerful portrait of Clytemnestra is that drawn by Electra in her first non-lyric speech. It is full of bitterness and made more effective by the use of mimicry (Euripides' Electra quotes Aegisthus (330-1) but only briefly):

> ...as if laughing at what she has done,
> when each month the day comes round
> on which she killed my father as a result of a trick,
> she celebrates with dances and sacrifices of sheep,
> making a monthly ceremony for the gods who have protected her!
> ...she, the woman so noble in her speech,
> addresses me and abuses me with curses such as this:
> "O ungodly pollution, are you the only one
> whose father has died?
> Is no other mortal suffering?
> Curses on you, may the gods below
> never release you from your present lamentations!"
> That's how she insults me...

$$(277-93)$$

When she appears in person Clytemnestra does not really live up to this description. She complains that Electra is defying her because Aegisthus is away and claims that her murder of Agamemnon was just retribution for the death of Iphigenia. If a child had to be sacrificed to enable the Greeks to set sail for Troy, why was it not one of Menelaus'? Electra rejects this and the two women quarrel; Clytemnestra loses her temper and threatens Electra with punishment 'when Aegisthus gets home' (627).

This Clytemnestra shows some apparently genuine emotion after the Tutor has described Orestes' 'death'. She tells the Tutor:

Motherhood is a strange thing:
not even one who has been treated badly
can hate one to whom she has given birth.

(770-1)

But she soon recovers her composure and revels in her freedom from
fear and the collapse of Electra's hopes. She describes Electra as if she
were the personification of a Fury:

She was the greater pest,
living with me and always draining my very life blood...

(784-6)

Some of those who believe that Sophocles wrote his *Electra* after
Euripides' version see his portrait of Clytemnestra as an attempt to
denigrate her in response to Euripides' more generous treatment.
However, the Queen in person does not match up to the vileness of
Electra's description, and it is Electra herself with her unrestrained
outpourings who seizes the audience's attention.

Euripides

Euripides' Electra is an even less sympathetic character than Sophocles'.
She churlishly rejects offers of kindness and seems totally engrossed in
self-martyrdom. The old Peasant, her husband, asks her to refrain from
fetching water as it is not suitable for one of noble birth, but she insists
on taking her share in the household tasks. The Peasant then remarks,
almost with bathos:

Go if it pleases you,
for the springs are not far from this hut.

(77-8)

Similarly, when the chorus women arrive and invite Electra to join them
at the festival of Hera, she immediately rejects their offer on the grounds
that she has nothing suitable to wear. The Chorus offer to lend her clothes
and jewelry and they remind her of the importance of honouring the gods
as well as indulging in mourning. But Electra will not be persuaded; she
seems determined to keep herself apart from the community. However,
in a later speech to the disguised Orestes she complains that she has no
share in festivals and is not allowed to join in the dancing (310).

Electra's hospitality towards strangers falls far short of that shown
by Clytemnestra in the other two plays and even of Aegisthus in this

version. She certainly does not match up to the Greek ideal of generosity towards strangers which forms an important theme of epics such as the *Odyssey*. The Peasant acts as a striking foil to her in this respect:

> These doors should have been opened long ago.
> Come into the house. In return for your good news you will receive
> whatever things fit for guests my house contains.
>
> (357-9)

This Electra is far more vituperative about Aegisthus than she is about her mother, a point which has led some commentators to suggest that Euripides intended to portray a frustrated and sexually jealous Electra. It is Aegisthus' insolence which she describes to the disguised Orestes:

> The man who murdered him...
> goes out in my father's chariot
> and seizes the sceptre with which he commanded the Greeks
> and flaunts it in his blood-stained hands...
> This glorious (so they say) husband of my mother,
> overcome with wine, jumps on my father's grave
> and pelts with stones my father's rocky monument.
>
> (319-28)

Later, Electra heaps abuse on Aegisthus' corpse, blaming him for Agamemnon's death, calling him a coward and hinting that he had other mistresses besides Clytemnestra – he was just a pretty face, not a real man at all! This is not supported by the report of Aegisthus' actual behaviour in the play. He is described as sacrificing reverently to the Nymphs and he warmly invites the passing strangers to join him at his rite.

Electra is unflattering in her descriptions of Clytemnestra, too, but not with the same venom which she directs towards Aegisthus. Once more appearances do not match her descriptions. Clytemnestra comes immediately when she hears that Electra has given birth. Her opening speech refers to Iphigenia, at once reminding the audience that she believed that she had cause to murder Agamemnon. She argues her case well, referring to the insult of sharing her husband with Cassandra and the double standards which pervaded relationships between men and women:

> Whenever the husband sins and puts aside his wife,
> the woman wants to copy the man and find another lover.

Then the blame blazes out on to us,
but the men, those who are responsible for the situation,
they are not badly thought of.
If Menelaus had been snatched secretly away from his home,
should I have killed Orestes
so that I might save Menelaus, my sister's husband?
How would your father have taken that?
Then why should he not have died, since he killed my daughter?
He would undoubtedly have killed me, if I had killed his son.
                                                                (1036-45)

Clytemnestra's response to Electra's further criticism is reminiscent of
Aeschylus' *Eumenides* where Athene claimed that she was 'always for
the man' (737). The Queen says:

Child, you always loved your father and it is still the case.
Some love their fathers,
but others love their mothers more than their fathers.
I forgive you.
Besides, I am not especially happy, child,
with the things that I have done.
                                                                (1102-6)

Indeed, the picture of Clytemnestra in Euripides' play is of a sadder and
wiser woman who is trying to be conciliatory rather than aggressive.
Nonetheless, true to the almost perversely contradictory spirit of Euripides' drama, once Clytemnestra has entered the hut to meet her death
the Chorus sing an ode about Agamemnon's murder, emphasising Clytemnestra's wickedness. They compare her to a fierce mountain lioness
(1163), an image which Aeschylus had used (*Agamemnon* 1258), but the
figure seen on stage seems far from being a lioness. Image and reality
are in conflict and heroism is entirely absent.

Conclusion

Aeschylus' *Libation Bearers* is primarily concerned with the place of
the murders of Clytemnestra and Aegisthus in the cycle of vengeance.
After the initial scene Electra is unimportant. Sophocles and Euripides
chose to give Electra a more prominent part in their plays. Sophocles'
drama is in many ways the tragedy of Electra. She is the pivot of the
play; once she has made her entry, except during the Tutor's *tour de force*
speech describing Orestes' death, it is Electra upon whom the audience's

attention is focused and in relation to whom all other characters are seen. Euripides' Electra also has a dominant role but his drama is more than just a play about Electra or about the vengeance taken on Clytemnestra and Aegisthus.

There is no common agreement about what Euripides intended: some claim that he was being literal-minded and prosaic, but Goldhill has argued quite persuasively that he was deliberately transgressing the conventions of dramatic representation. It is a play about the perversion of rituals and the social order: Aegisthus is murdered while sacrificing to the gods, Clytemnestra when invited to a sacrifice; the king's daughter has been married to a peasant, but is still a virgin; the Peasant proves to have more nobility of spirit than any of the noble-born characters; a choral ode about the hero Achilles is juxtaposed to a scene involving an unheroic Orestes outside a peasant's hut; the Chorus sing about Thyestes and the golden lamb and then remark that they cannot believe such stories; recognition tokens are introduced only to be rejected; descriptions of characters fail to match the appearance of the characters themselves; there is no triumph at the end, merely remorse, doubt and disgust.

Above all, these three versions of the same episode show that it was the playwright's skill as a presenter of visual effects, as a poet and as an interpreter of differing aspects of the myth, rather than the original story itself which was paramount.

Suggestions for Further Study

Chapter 1. Make a list of the ways in which the performance of an ancient Greek tragedy differed from that of a play today. Why might only three actors have ever been used in tragedy? Try to work out which actor played which parts in the tragedy you are currently studying. What differences might wearing a mask make to an actor's performance?

Chapter 2. Try to imagine the atmosphere at the City Dionysia: could it be described as religious? Which aspects of the festival seem to have been most important to the Athenians? What modern event might it be compared to?

Chapter 3. What other recurrent images occur in the *Oresteia*? Are there any other examples of irony or 'double-speak'? What purpose does the old nurse Cilissa serve in the *Libation Bearers*? Does the tone of her speech seem to be consistent with that of the rest of the play? Evaluate the case made for and against Orestes in the trial scene of the *Eumenides*; should he have been acquitted? Does Orestes seem to be a heroic character?

Chapter 4. Does the *Antigone* justify the assertion that the best tragedies involve not a single tragic hero but a plurality of tragic characters? What other examples of irony are there in the two plays which are discussed? What other recurrent images are to be found in the *Antigone*? Would the Athenian audience have felt more sympathy for Oedipus in the *Oedipus Tyrannus* than for Creon in the *Antigone*?

Chapter 5. Does the evidence of the plays suggest that Euripides was an atheist? Could he justifiably be called a woman-hater? Would the Athenian audience have felt more sympathy for Jason or for Medea? What impression of Theseus is conveyed by the *Hippolytus*? Was Dionysus justified in acting as he did in the *Bacchae*?

Chapter 6. Which version of the Electra story do you prefer? Why? Did Clytemnestra have any just grounds for her actions? Does Orestes emerge honourably from any of the three plays?

Suggestions for Further Reading

Goldhill, S., *Reading Greek Tragedy* (Cambridge, CUP, 1986). A scholarly book, but one aimed at the Greekless reader. It puts tragedy firmly within Athenian society as well as dealing with the language of tragedy in detail.

Knox, B., *The Heroic Temper: Studies in Sophoclean Tragedy* (Berkeley, University of California Press, 1964). A study of the Sophoclean hero. Its thesis is controversial in part but it includes a detailed examination of the plays.

Rosenmeyer, T., *The Art of Aeschylus* (Berkeley, University of California Press, 1982). A very readable, if rather dogmatic, analysis of the extant plays of Aeschylus.

Segal, C., *Interpreting Greek Tragedy: Myth, Poetry, Text* (Ithaca and London, Cornell University Press, 1986). A stimulating selection of essays, mostly about language and symbolism, adopting a structuralist approach. A challenging volume.

Segal, E. (ed.), *Oxford Readings in Greek Tragedy* (Oxford, OUP, 1983). An interesting collection of essays on a wide variety of topics by some twenty of the leading scholars in the field.

Taplin, O., *Greek Tragedy in Action* (London, Methuen, 1978). A lively and detailed examination of the performance of Greek tragedy, covering aspects such as spectacle, entrances and exits, and props.

Vellacott, P., *Ironic Drama: a Study of Euripides' Method and Meaning* (Cambridge, CUP, 1975). A very idiosyncratic study of Euripides; nonetheless, it contains lots of interesting ideas.

Winnington-Ingram, R., *Sophocles: An Interpretation* (Cambridge, CUP, 1980). A clearly written and easily intelligible book. Some of the ideas are controversial but it is stimulating to read.

Winnington-Ingram, R., *Studies in Aeschylus* (Cambridge, CUP, 1983). Controversial in places, but this book deals with all of the main points of Aeschylean scholarship in an accessible manner.

Morals and Values in Ancient Greece
John Ferguson

From the society of the Homeric poems through to the rise of Christianity, this account charts the progression of morals and values in the Greek world.

The author begins by discussing how a 'guilt-culture' superseded the old 'shame-culture' without totally displacing it. He then examines how democracy, the philosophers and finally Alexander's conquest influenced the values of the ancient Greeks.

Original texts are quoted in translation, and this clear, chronological study will provide an exciting introduction for students while offering experts a fresh approach to the subject.

Slavery in Classical Greece
N.R.E. Fisher

This is an authoritative and clearly written account of the main issues involved in the study of Greek slavery from Homeric times to the fourth century BC. It provides valuable insights into the fundamental place of slavery in the economies and social life of classical Greece, and includes penetrating analyses of the widely-held ancient ideological justifications of slavery.

A wide range of topics is covered, including chapters on the development of slavery from Homer to the classical period, on the peculiar form of community slaves (the helots) found in Sparta, on the economic functions and the treatment of slaves in Athens, and on the evidence for slaves' resistance. Throughout, the book shows how political and economic systems, ideas of national identity, work and gender, and indeed the fundamental nature of Greek civilization itself, were all profoundly affected by the fact that many of the Greek city-states were slave societies.

Classical Epic: Homer and Virgil
Richard Jenkyns

In the ancient world Homer was recognised as the fountain-head of culture. His poems, the *Iliad* and the *Odyssey*, were universally admired as examples of great literature which could never be surpassed.

In this new study, Richard Jenkyns re-examines the two Homeric epics and the work that is perhaps their closest rival, the *Aeneid* of Virgil. A wide range of topics is covered, including chapters on heroism and tragedy in the *Iliad*, morality in the *Odyssey* and Virgil's skilful reworking of elements from the two earlier epics.

Greece and the Persians
John Sharwood Smith

This account traces each stage of the critical struggle between the Persian Empire and the early Greek states, from the first clashes to the miraculous return home of 10,000 Greek mercenaries stranded in the heart of Persia.

Carefully examining sources and placing events within their geographical and historical contexts, the author attempts to define cultural and political differences between the two peoples. His balanced questioning approach places fresh emphasis on the Persian perspective and will provide an accessible and informed introduction to the period.

Athens Under the Tyrants
J.A. Smith

This study focuses on the colourful period of the Peisistratid tyranny in Athens. During these exciting years the great festivals were established, monumental buildings were erected, the population grew rapidly and there was lively progress in all the arts.

This study considers the artistic, archaeological and literary evidence for the period. Athens is seen largely through the eyes of Herodotus, the 'Father of History', and we can observe the foundations being laid for the growth of democracy in the following century.

Greek Architecture
R.A. Tomlinson

Greek Architecture is a clearly structured discussion of all the major buildings constructed by the Greeks, from houses to temples, theatres to Council buildings.

This book describes particular architectural styles and features and sets the buildings in their context, with an evaluation of their purpose, siting and planning.

With over 40 illustrations enhancing the text, *Greek Architecture* provides an informed and comprehensive view of the design and function of buildings in ancient Greece.

Augustan Rome
Andrew Wallace-Hadrill

This highly illustrated introduction to Rome in the Age of Augustus provides a fascinating insight into the social and physical contexts of Augustan politics and poetry, taking a detailed look at the impact of the new regime of government on society.

The ideas and environment manipulated by Augustus are explored, along with reactions to that manipulation.

Unlike more standard works on Augustus, this book places greater emphasis on the art and architecture of the time, and on Roman attitudes and values.

The Julio-Claudian Emperors
Thomas Wiedemann

'The dark, unrelenting Tiberius, the furious Caligula, the feeble Claudius, the profligate and cruel Nero...are condemned to everlasting infamy' wrote Gibbon. This 'infamy' has inspired the work of historians and novelists from Roman times to the present.

This book summarises political events during the reigns of Tiberius, Caligula, Claudius and Nero, and the civil wars of the 'year of four emperors'. It considers too the extent to which social factors influenced the imperial household.

Assuming no knowledge of Latin and drawing on material including inscriptions and coins, literary history and the latest historical interpretations, the author presents a coherent account of the often apparently erratic actions of these emperors.